THE BIG ONE-OH

THE BIG ONE-OH

DEAN PITCHFORD

G. P. PUTNAM'S SONS

G. P. PUTNAM'S SONS

A division of Penguin Young Readers Group. Published by The Penguin Group.
Penguin Group (USA) Inc., 375 Hudson Street, New York, NY 10014, U.S.A.
Penguin Group (Canada), 90 Eglinton Avenue East, Suite 700, Toronto, Ontario,
Canada M4P 2Y3 (a division of Pearson Penguin Canada Inc.). Penguin Books Ltd,
80 Strand, London WC2R 0RL, England. Penguin Ireland, 25 St. Stephen's Green,
Dublin 2, Ireland (a division of Penguin Books Ltd.). Penguin Group (Australia),
250 Camberwell Road, Camberwell, Victoria 3124, Australia (a division of Pearson
Australia Group Pty Ltd). Penguin Books India Pvt Ltd, 11 Community Centre,
Panchsheel Park, New Delhi—110 017, India. Penguin Group (NZ), Cnr Airborne and
Rosedale Roads, Albany, Auckland 1310, New Zealand (a division of Pearson New
Zealand Ltd). Penguin Books (South Africa) (Pty) Ltd, 24 Sturdee Avenue, Rosebank,
Johannesburg 2196, South Africa. Penguin Books Ltd, Registered Offices: 80 Strand,
London WC2R 0RL, England.

Printed in the United States of America.

Design by Gunta Alexander. Text set in Alinea Medium.

Library of Congress Cataloging-in-Publication Data
Pitchford, Dean.
The big one-oh / Dean Pitchford.
p. cm.
Summary: Determined not to be weird all his life like his neighbor, Charley
Maplewood decides to throw himself a tenth birthday party, complete with a "house
of horrors" theme, but first he will have to make some friends to invite.
[1. Birthdays—Fiction. 2. Parties—Fiction. 3. Single-parent families—Fiction.
4. Self-actualization (Psychology)—Fiction.] I. Title.
PZ7.P644Big 2007
[Fic]—dc22
2006014266

ISBN 978-0-399-24547-3
10 9 8 7 6 5 4 3 2 1
First Impression

TO PATRICIA,
WHO WAS THE LIFE OF EVERY PARTY

My name is Charley Maplewood, and I'm 10.

Ten years old.

Today.

You'd think it would be a truly awesome event. An exciting turning point. I mean, come on!

TEN YEARS OLD!

That's a *monumental moment* in the life of a kid, *right?!*

Ha ha.

I mean, just look at what I've done in the last few weeks: I've shocked and embarrassed my family. I've left a trail of destruction and chaos in my path. And I've ruined what was left of my pathetic little life.

I've made such a big, rotten stinking mess of everything that I'll bet some people are surprised I even lived to see this day.

But I've got good reasons for everything I did.

I can explain.

Really.

But to do that, I have to tell you about a package I got a month ago. From my dad.

And I'm not blaming him, but I swear that, if it weren't for that package, none of this would have ever happened.

DAD'S
TEN WORDS

1

The day Dad's package came, I skateboarded home from school as usual. I could probably get home faster if I walked, because I always fall off my skateboard about five hundred times on the way; but, when I started skateboarding at the beginning of this school year, I used to fall off about a thousand times, so that's progress, isn't it?

I slid and skidded up our driveway and finally crashed on the front lawn, and then I let my dog Boing Boing out of the side yard where he sleeps and scratches himself all day.

Boing Boing is a big mutt. I would never have named him—or *any* dog—Boing Boing, but he started out as Mom's dog. He sleeps in my bed, so he's really more *my* dog now, but Mom won't change his name. So guess who gets stuck running around the neighborhood, yelling, "Boing Boing! C'mere, Boing Boing!"?

I sound like a video game.

That day Boing Boing flew out of the side yard gate like he always does, and he knocked me down with his wet kisses and huge paws. That's why I didn't hear Mrs. Cleveland coming, and why I jumped when she suddenly snapped, *"Child?!"*

Mrs. Cleveland is the plump, old, African-American lady who lives next door. She wears black socks with white tennis shoes, and she spends her days walking up and down the block jiggling other people's doorknobs and making sure that garages and mailboxes are firmly shut.

I sat up on the lawn and squinted up at her.

"Huh?"

"Is your daddy still overseas?" she demanded.

"I, uhhhh . . . he's in Scotland. Glasgow, Scotland. It's the capital," I stammered.

"Well, that's overseas," she sniffed. "You're gonna wanna check your mail, then," she said before she turned and marched off, using one of her late husband's golf clubs as a walking stick.

As usual, Mrs. Cleveland was right: I had gotten a large envelope from Dad, covered with lots of colorful Scottish stamps.

Whenever Dad sends a letter or something, I always spend a moment studying the stamps, trying to imagine what the post office looked like where Dad bought them and licked them and stuck them on. I try to picture what the weather might be like over there and where Dad goes after he drops my package into the mail slot.

Most days, I know, he goes to the restaurant where he cooks, because he's a chef. A really good one, too. My dad can cook *anything*. The place he works in Glasgow, Scotland, is a Mexican café, and, even though he's not Mexican, he told me that the Scottish people are starved for good Mexican food.

At least that's what he said when he left home three years ago. I try not to think about that day.

In my bedroom, Boing Boing sniffed and licked at Dad's package until I opened up the big, puffy envelope. Inside, wrapped in blue paper that said "Happy Birthday!!" all over was a flat parcel that I figured out was supposed to be my birthday present.

Four weeks early.

Dad's usually within a month or two. He never remembers my exact birth *day*, but that's okay. I bet he's got a lot on his mind.

I immediately knew what was in the wrapping paper because Dad always sends me the same present: two issues of *Monsters & Maniacs.*

What?!

You've never heard of *Monsters & Maniacs?* What planet did you grow up on? It's only the greatest literature in the history of the world!

Monsters & Maniacs is a comic book all about zombies and vampires and madmen and stuff. It's got demons (like in Issue 113: "The Gates of Hell Are *UNDER MY BED!!*"), giant spiders (Issue 49: "Six Hairy Legs and *SIX FEET TALL!!*"), aliens (Issue 85: "On My Planet *YOU'D BE LUNCH!!*"), and the occasional headless babysitter (Issue 136: "What Have You Done *WITH MY CHILDREN?!*").

I loved them even before I could read the words, because the pictures were just so cool. Then, when we learned the alphabet in first grade, I'd run home from school every day and practice reading them.

My happiest memories always involve *Monsters & Maniacs.* Back when Dad was still living here, for instance, I used to grab a stack of issues and read that stack from top to bottom. Afterward I'd go downstairs, and Dad would grill me a cheese sandwich. And he'd let me flip it on the griddle.

Those were good times.

* * *

I wasn't in any hurry to open up Dad's issues of *Monster &*
Maniacs, because I knew I had them already. I get every issue
the moment it hits the racks at The Comic Soup, the store
where I spend all my allowance.

Instead I opened the card that was taped to the present.
On the cover, above a picture of a boy sailing a boat, it said,
"Oh, good heaven! You're going to be eleven!"

"Ten, Dad. I'm going to be ten," I groaned as if he were in
the room with me. Then I opened the card and read where
he had written, "Happy Birthday, Charley!"

And below that he had scribbled the ten words that
kicked off this whole horrible chain of events:

"What are you going to do for your big day?"

2

As soon as I read Dad's words, my heart flipped over in my chest. My hands started to shake. I could feel myself growing short of breath. Because thinking about what people do on birthdays—mine or anyone else's—always makes me remember something that happened three and a half years ago.

Something that scarred me for life and still causes me to wake up screaming.

I was invited to my first birthday party ever.

I was six.

We had just moved onto Apple Core Circle because my dad got hired to be the chef at the nearby Wagon Wheel Family-Style Restaurant. Dad and Mom argued a lot where we lived before, so I guess maybe they thought that a change of location might help them get along. Or a new job would help. Or something like that. I didn't pay a lot of attention then.

Soon after we'd moved in, I got invited to this kid Jamie Wiggerty's birthday party; I'd never even met the guy. One day Mom stopped to chat with his mother in the middle of the Pic 'n' Save, and the next thing I know, Mom's gushing, "Charley would *love* to come!"

She didn't even consult me.

When I pointed that out to Mom on the way home, she laughed, "C'mon, Charley! This'll help you make some new friends."

"That's so totally lame," sneered my sister Lorena once she heard the news. Lorena was twelve at the time, and she thought that *every*thing *every*body *ever* did *any*where at *any* time was totally lame.

She still thinks that.

Dad was more enthusiastic. "You'll have a blast," he assured me.

So I went.

Dad walked me to Jamie Wiggerty's house that terrible Saturday morning. The backyard was filled with lots of parents and kids, and when Dad saw some adults he knew, I was left alone to look around.

In the center of the lawn, on a gigantic picnic table, sat the biggest cake I'd ever seen, a humongous bowl of pink punch and piles of presents. There were streamers draped between all the trees, and kids were all running around, blowing noisemakers and swatting at balloons.

There was even a man giving all the kids pony rides, but the pony clip-clopped around his temporary corral so slowly that it looked like about as much fun as watching paint dry.

And, just as I'd figured, I didn't know anyone. So it was a good thing I had smuggled in some comic books.

"Geez, Charley! Can't you go one day without *Monsters & Maniacs*?" Dad groaned when he found me by myself, reading under a tree. "And your mother wonders why you have no friends."

Now, I had never heard it put that way before. First of all, I had never really stopped to think about it, but, yeah, I had no friends. But, hey, I was six; I figured I had time.

And second, I never realized that it was something Mom and Dad would even notice—me not having friends. I thought they had plenty of other things to worry about.

Dad stuck a curly party-favor noisemaker in my mouth, took me by the hand and led me across the lawn to the corral as Jamie and his friends watched.

The Pony Man squinted through the smoke of his stinky cigar as Dad lifted me up and set me down in the saddle. "You're the last one to ride the pony, Kiddo," Dad said.

I got the feeling that the pony wasn't too happy to have yet another squirming kid on his back. I totally sympathized; I wasn't thrilled to be there, either. But it seemed important to Dad that I give it a shot.

"See?" said Dad. "Nice horsie. Hang on, Charley."

He didn't have to tell me that; I gripped those reins so tightly my hands turned white.

"Say 'Giddyap!' " Dad urged. "The horsie won't go until you say, 'Giddyap, horsie.' "

Thanks, Dad. That was all Jamie and his friends needed to hear. They began to shout, "Giddyap!" "Say 'Giddyap, horsie!' " "Make the horsie giddyap, giddyap, *GIDDYAP!!*"

They got louder and louder, stomping their feet and screeching like chimpanzees. While the Pony Man was blowing cigar smoke my way, Dad kept urging, "Say 'Giddyap!,' Charley! 'Giddyap!' " and trying to yank the noisemaker from between my clamped, gritting teeth.

Can you understand how I could get confused?

I took a deep breath which I fully intended to use to say, "Giddyap!" Instead, I blew powerfully into the noisemaker, which made an awfully loud honk.

Which the pony didn't like one bit.

Not only that, but the curled-up party-favor uncurled, and the little feather at the end of it must've tickled him in a place that he didn't like to be tickled. Because that pony threw back his head, whinnied like he was being poked with a burning torch, reared back on his hind legs and then, while I hung on for dear life, he—I mean, *we*—took off like a shot.

BAM!

That pony and I plowed through his flimsy little corral. We rocketed across the lawn—with Dad and the Pony Man chasing us—and we trampled Mrs. Wiggerty's perfect flower beds. We zigged this way, and we zagged over there, galloping straight for clumps of kids, who ran, shrieking, in every direction.

Parents began chasing us, too. They were slipping on the grass, crashing into chairs and smashing into each other. They were waving their arms and screaming out suggestions: "Say, 'Whoa!' " "Pull his reins!" "Grab his bridle!"

Then, suddenly, everybody seemed to get organized and formed two lines. The kids and parents were closing in on us, cutting off our escape. They formed a single path that led right up to the picnic table, where they knew we'd have to stop, because there was no way the pony could gallop fast enough and leap high enough to clear that picnic table.

Was there?

Later, the Pony Man would tell Dad that, in all the time

he owned him, he had never seen his pony leap so high before.

Sadly, it wasn't high enough.

It amazes me to this day that the pony and I both walked
away from the crash without a scratch. Oh, sure, we were
covered with cake and frosting and punch and birthday candles and ribbons and wrapping paper.

And, yeah, there were hot dogs and presents and potato
chips and pickles scattered as far as the eye could see.

Jamie Wiggerty was crying into his mother's dress, and
when they saw that, a few other kids started sobbing, too.

So Dad and I left real fast.

I never pinned a tail on a donkey, I never got to eat ice
cream and cake, and I never sang *"Happy Birthday, dear Ja—
mie!!"*

And after that, I never got invited to another
birthday party.

I shook off that horrible memory and steadied my trembling
hand, in which I was still gripping Dad's birthday card. To
ease my panic, I read his message out loud:

"What are you going to do for your big day?"

And when I realized what I had just asked, I gasped, "Wait
a minute!"

That made Boing Boing look up.

"It *IS* my big day!" Boing Boing tilted his head in drowsy
confusion and went back to sleep, but my mind was racing
with this startling new understanding:

I was gonna turn ten. Me. Charley Maplewood. Ten years old. No more single-digit birthdays—1, 2, 3, 4, 5, 6, 7, 8, 9.

NO!

I would finally move into double digits—*and then I'd never go back again.*

How awesome was that? Life-changing, even.

I began to think that maybe it was time to put the disaster of Jamie Wiggerty's birthday party behind me.

Maybe it was time to move on.

Maybe I *should* do something for my "big day."

But what?

3

Later that afternoon when Mom came home from work, I watched her closely and decided to wait a few minutes before starting a conversation.

See, Mom's the bookkeeper at Fittipaldi's Appliances, where they sell stoves and TVs and vacuum cleaners. Even though she gets a whopping twenty percent employee discount on anything in the store, she also has to deal with Mr. Fittipaldi, who can be very . . . loud. Mom never speaks badly about Mr. Fittipaldi's temper, but I can always tell if she's had "one of those days."

If Mom groans when she pulls off her shoes and shakes her head as she flips through the mail, I know that I should wait before I open my mouth. But if she notices what I'm cooking for dinner and she sniffs at the pots on the stove and goes, "Mmmm, smells good," as soon as she walks in, then it's a pretty safe bet that I can ask her anything.

That day, I decided to wait. And, while I waited, I continued chopping parsley.

People find it strange that I do the cooking in our house, but I don't see why. After all, Dad's a cook. I watched him a lot before he was gone. He left behind lots of great pots and pans and spoons and things, but he took his favorite knives with him.

Without any help, I can reach the front burners on the

stove. For now, I still need to stand on a kitchen chair to reach the back burners, but, if I keep growing on schedule, I should be tall enough to do that by next summer.

And besides, if I left it up to Mom, we'd have chili dogs 365 days a year, so doing all the cooking is really more out of self-defense.

After Mom unpinned her hair and shook it out, I sensed that it was finally okay to speak, so I asked her what she had planned for my "big day."

"Your 'big day'?" She blinked.

"My birthday."

"Oh, honey! Your birthday's not for a month. We've got time."

Just then Lorena came barging in the front door. My sister's in tenth grade now, and she's still a pain.

At that time, she had a job after school at the Chick-A-Dee Restaurant, selling fried chicken and coleslaw and sodas. I had a feeling she was only working there because of Brad, her supervisor, who is seventeen and has lots of spiky black hair. The way he'd zip around the Chick-A-Dee kitchen shouting orders into his little "talk-to-me-People!" headset had convinced Lorena that Brad was the coolest thing since ice cream.

Lorena walked in on my discussion with Mom just as I said, "But Dad sent me a birthday card, and he wants to know what I'm doing for my 'big day,' and I don't know what to tell him."

Lorena made a little snorting laugh. "Why's Dad sending you a birthday card this early? Man, he sucks with dates."

I think Lorena is still really angry with Dad for leaving. She sneers whenever she says his name in public, but sometimes I hear her and Mom whispering behind her bedroom door late at night. And when they do, Lorena's usually crying, so I know better than to stick my head in and ask, "Hey, what's up?"

Lorena scrunched up her nose as she passed by me and glanced at what I was cooking. "Sloppy Joes?" she asked.

I shook my head. "Lamb curry with spinach."

She groaned. "There's never anything to eat in this house."

It was then that Mom first noticed I had a stove full of bubbling pans and pots. She whirled around to my sister. "Lorena!"

"What?"

"Didn't you give your brother my message?"

"I'm not your secretary," Lorena muttered.

That steamed Mom. "I gave you a cell phone for emergencies, so when I call and ask you to tell your brother that I won't be here for dinner . . ."

"Well, I'm sorry," huffed Lorena, "but Brad called me to do an extra shift at the Chick-A-Dee, so I had other things on my mind, okay?"

Mom opened her mouth to answer, but then she thought better of it, so she just took a deep breath and turned to me.

"I'm sorry, sweetie. I have a date tonight."

"Oh?" I asked. As if I didn't know what was coming.

"Yeah. Vince is taking me for Szechuan."

Lorena rolled her eyes and groaned.

And, although I didn't say anything, that was pretty much how I felt, too.

Mom met Vince Champagne a couple months ago at some fancy-dancy market he manages called The Paradise Pantry. Mom went there to get a deli platter for a party at work, and Vince was pricing cheeses in the dairy cabinet when Mom walked by. They started talking about imported cheddar and California Swiss and the next thing you know, they were going out.

Now, I realize that Mom is probably lonely. Actually, I know she is. More than once I've come downstairs after midnight to find her still up, doing her crossword puzzle or blowing on a hot cup of tea and staring across the living room. She always assures me, "No, nothing's wrong," but I'll bet she'd like someone else to talk to besides me and Lorena and Mr. Fittipaldi.

But why Vince? He's got a thick neck, like he must've played football at one time . . . until he decided that he'd rather stack vegetables in pyramid-shaped piles. He's the kind of guy who slaps people on the back when he meets them and then laughs too close to their face. He'd always grab my hand, squeeze it and shout, "C'mon, Charley! Gimme a *man's* handshake!"

It made me nuts.

Mom wanted to change the subject from Vince, so she suddenly came up with, "You know what, Charley? I just remembered: your sister had a party . . ." She turned to Lorena. "Didn't you? When you turned ten?"

Lorena was chewing on an ice cube. "You mean at our old house? The time when the sprinklers went off, and me and my girlfriends all got covered in mud and grass, and so you hosed us down in our party dresses? That time?"

Mom decided not to relive that memory.

"Well," she bubbled, "your brother might want a party."

Lorena screwed up her face. "Why? Who would he invite?"

"It's up to him," said Mom.

"But he doesn't have any friends," Lorena insisted.

"Don't say that!" Mom hissed, as she left the kitchen.

Lorena followed her, protesting, "Well, he *doesn't*." She didn't even care that I could hear her.

Then Mom popped her head back in the kitchen door.

"Honey? You've got friends, right?"

The way that she asked it, biting on her lower lip with just a hint of worry in her eyes, made me realize that it must be important to her.

"Sure do," I smiled. And I went back to stirring my lamb curry.

She exhaled, winked at me, and went upstairs to get ready for Vince.

The question that she raised, though, was an interesting one. I decided that it was worth further study.

4

For the next few days, I started to look at people at school, *really* look at them as if for the first time, and ask myself, *Charley? Can you call this person a friend?*

I didn't like the answer I kept coming up with.

For instance, during math class on Tuesday, when Mr. Jordan sent me and three other kids to the blackboard to solve square root problems, I looked out, and I saw Donna Pointer, who is too beautiful to describe.

Donna looked up from her math paper, and her straight brown hair bouncing off her shoulders made her teeth seem unbelievably . . . *white.* I guess I stopped to look, because, when she she saw me, she smiled a little smile.

I'm not making this up.

Now, sometimes Donna would nod to me in the hallway if we passed each other and our eyes met.

And there was this one day last year when she asked to borrow a pencil from me before a spelling quiz, and when she returned it at the end of class she said, "Thanks a bunch, Charley." So I knew she knew my name.

Wow. For the first time, I wondered, *Is Donna Pointer maybe my friend?*

Donna pals around with two other girls, Dina Andrews and Dana McGuire. They're nice enough, I guess, but if you think of Donna as the sun, then Dina and Dana are more like moons, orbiting around her.

When I caught Donna's eye, I shrugged, sort of like, *"Square roots? Hey. No problem."* And I gave a little wink.

I guess Dina and Dana saw the wink, because they started to giggle. I could feel my face redden as I turned back to the blackboard, determined to solve my square roots with the speed and style that would earn Donna's admiration. But, in my hurry, I scraped the chalk across the board, and it made that horrible squeaky noise that makes everyone who hears it inhale sharply.

Then, even worse, my chalk broke, my hand slipped, and I made a long slash that wasn't part of my square root solution. By this time, there were more snickers.

So I picked up the eraser to neaten my work, but when I swiped it across the blackboard, the eraser took a skittering skip, flipped out of my hand and flew over my head onto Mr. Jordan's desk, where it landed with a *poof!* of chalk dust on his lesson plan.

That got everybody laughing—everybody except Mr. Jordan.

Now, I'm used to being embarrassed—just skateboarding off school property is bad enough—so I squeezed my lips together real tight and retrieved the eraser. But before I turned back to the board, I looked once more at Donna; by now she had joined Dina and Dana in laughing and covering their mouths like they had chewed food that they didn't want anybody to see.

I wasn't sure if that's what a friend would do.

* * *

In the elementary school, the boys' room on the ground floor is where most guys go, but it gets so crowded that sometimes, in the crush, I end up getting shoved into the paper towel dispenser or having the water faucet stream directed at me. So I tend to visit the boys' room on the second floor; it's way smaller, but it's not as risky.

I usually run into Darryl Egbert there. Darryl's the smartest guy in fourth grade, but he can be unpredictable.

Darryl sweats a lot and worries about his grades a lot, and his mother takes him to see a psychology doctor once a week because he gets stomach cramps and sometimes he can't sleep at night. But he knows all the answers in every subject. Whenever he's called on, Darryl pushes his glasses back against his nose and sticks his hands under his armpits before he speaks. Then he almost shouts, and the veins on his neck bulge. So people tend to treat Darryl in that careful way you see in movies about people defusing a bomb.

But when we see each other in the upstairs boys' room, we usually say, "Hey." And whenever I put my tray down next to his in the cafeteria, he never tells me to beat it; sometimes he'll even look up from the book he's reading and say something like, "Do you realize that cow flatulence is responsible for twenty-five percent of the methane gas in our atmosphere?"

So later that week in the boys' room I didn't think it was out of place for me to ask him, "Darryl? Would you say that you and me are friends?"

He looked up from the sink, where he was splashing water

on his face. He does that when he gets overheated, and he gets overheated when he's nervous about something.

" 'You and *I*,' " he corrected me.

"Huh?" I blinked.

" '*Me*' is objective, '*I*' is nominative. The question is 'Would you say that you and *I* are friends?' "

"Yeah," I nodded. "Would you?"

"What? *Friends?*" That seemed to totally confuse him. "I . . . *what?* Why are you asking me that *now?!* We've got an American history quiz in seven minutes, and this is neither the time nor the . . . urp . . . !"

The "urp!" was because he was about to throw up, but he didn't do that in the sink; he rushed into one of the stalls and slammed the door and heaved.

So I couldn't really count that as a "yes."

The next day, on my way to geography, I saw Leo Jacobi down the hall. Leo's a good guy. Everybody thinks so.

Earlier this year, when Leo was running for Class President, I got into line behind him one day after recess, and I tapped him on the shoulder and said, "You've got my vote."

And you know what he did? He turned around and shook my hand and patted me on the shoulder. But he didn't say anything because we're not supposed to talk after the recess bell.

Of course, he won; he always does. Nobody's ever dumb enough to run against him.

So that afternoon in the hallway, when Leo looked up and saw me, he raised a hand and waved, "Hey."

I froze, not sure whether to return the gesture. *Is Leo really waving to me?* I wondered. But then I answered myself, *Well, why wouldn't he? Leo's a friendly guy.* Which of course led to the big question, *Does that make him a friend?*

Just in case it did, I lifted my hand to wave back at the same moment that a bunch of guys came from behind me and raced over to surround Leo and clap him on the back.

That's who Leo was waving to.

I stood there stupidly, with my hand in midair. Rather than waste the wave, I made a swoop and brought my hand down on the button of the drinking fountain.

Yeah, I thought. *Perfect timing. I need a drink.*

Except that just as I took my first sip—WHAM!—I got smacked on the side of the head, and as I stumbled back, I heard, *"Leave some for me!"*

It could only be one person.

"OW! Leland!" I sputtered, and the water spurted out of my mouth and onto the hallway tiles.

Leland Plunk has been on my case ever since I tranferred to this school. Leland has wild hair, messy clothes, and crooked teeth; he looks like somebody put him into a clothes dryer once, tumbled him around for a while, and then shoved him out the door. He's about my height, which makes him too short to pick on the bigger guys, so he decided a long time ago that I was just the right size to torture.

Leland stuck his face into mine and hollered, "Hey! What'd I tell you?! It's no longer 'Leland.' Don't call me 'Leland' anymore."

"Oh, right. What's the new name? I keep forgetting," I said.

Leland snarled over his shoulder, "What's my name, Scottie?"

Scottie Heep is so thick and squat that when he puts his fists on his hips you could mistake him for a fire hydrant. I think Scottie would really *like* to get into more trouble than he does, but he can't figure out how, so he hangs around with Leland, who is really full of rotten, mean ideas.

" 'Cougar'!" Scottie announced. "It's 'Cougar' now."

Leland backed me up against the wall. "Can you say that? 'Cougar.' Say it. 'Cooooo-ger.' "

In that moment, I actually stopped to think: *What if I did? What if I called Leland "Cougar"? Would he stop smacking me around? Would he like me, even a little bit?*

And would that mean we were friends? Me and Cougar?

And, of course, Scottie would be included as part of the deal.

Wow. TWO friends. Just by saying one word. It was worth a shot.

But before I could speak, someone behind Leland . . . I mean, *Cougar* . . . asked: "Do you even know how to *spell* 'cougar'?"

I recognized that voice. Unfortunately.

Leland turned very slowly.

Jennifer Mobley's braces glinted under the fluorescent bulbs overhead.

Now, if anybody ever gave Jennifer a nickname, it would have to be "Red," because she's so . . . *red*. She's got red freckles all over her pinkish face, she's got red eyelashes, and she's got curly red hair that looks like it exploded out of her skull one day and she never managed to pull it back in.

But people don't give nicknames to people like Jennifer and me, unless they're the kinds of nicknames that you'd really rather not have.

"Your name is 'Leland,' " Jennifer explained to him, as if she were talking to a puppy. " 'Cougar' is just plain dumb."

Cougar looked her up and down for a moment.

"Did you save the receipt?" he asked.

Jennifer played right into his sneaky little hands. "What receipt?"

"The one for your face," he crowed. "Cuz once you look in a mirror, you're gonna want to return this one for a refund!"

He and Scottie split a gut laughing at that as they ran off down the hall, leaving me to face Jennifer. Alone.

Jennifer got the idea in second grade that, because she likes *Monsters & Maniacs* too, we were soul mates or something creepy like that.

She held up the latest issue. "Did you find the Chalice of Satan hidden on this month's cover?" she gushed, and little dots of her saliva flew every which way.

Since I always keep my copies of *Monsters & Maniacs*—and the extras Dad sends me—in perfect condition and store them in airtight plastic bins under my bed, arranged by date of issue, it's always horrifying to see how Jennifer scribbles and draws all over hers. And she does it *every month*.

It's madness.

So I didn't even answer her. I just grunted and rolled my eyes, as if to say, *"I'm too cool for that."*

And I walked away.

5

As I kept falling off my skateboard on the way home, I reviewed the week in my head.

I couldn't really say that there was anybody in school who I could call a friend. And certainly nobody who would call me a friend.

Except Jennifer, and I didn't even want to be *seen* with her.

But is that so bad—not having friends? I wondered. *After all, I've got school. I've got Boing Boing and Monsters & Maniacs and making dinner every night. My life is full,* I told myself. *Even if it does get a little lonely sometimes.*

Whoa.

"Lonely"?

How did that sneak in there?

I hadn't thought of it before, but, yeah, it gets lonely. Then, before I could get too upset about that realization, I saw something that made me fall off my skateboard again.

It was our neighbor Garry Quarky. Down on his knees on the sidewalk. With his head stuck in the bushes that separate his yard from ours.

It was only the second time I had ever seen the guy who lives right next door.

Garry Quarky moved into the house on the other side of us from Mrs. Cleveland about five months ago. Mom baked chocolate chip cookies and left them on his porch to welcome him to the neighborhood, but he never came over to say, "thank you."

"What an odd man," I remember Mom said at the time.

We knew Garry had a girlfriend who Lorena called "Pincushion" because she had earrings and spikes and hoops in her ears and her nose and her lips and her eyelids.

I'm serious.

I used to see Pincushion drive up and park her big old boat of a convertible in Garry's driveway every afternoon and carry groceries into his house, but I had only seen Garry come out once before.

That happened one afternoon when I was home alone, and I suddenly heard a horrifying *shriek* from next door. After I jumped about five feet off the ground, I ran into Lorena's room, because her windows look out over Garry's backyard, and this is what I saw:

Garry came dashing out of his house screaming, "Aiyeeeee!" and wearing a rubber apron and goggles, like maybe a mad scientist would wear. He looked like he was about as old as my mom, but it was hard to tell since his long hair was hanging down in his face and over his glasses. He had on thick gloves and, from hand to hand, he was tossing a test tube that was spitting fire and sparks. He kept yelling, "Hot! Hot! Hot!" as he ran across the lawn to an old concrete birdbath that was filled up with green scummy rainwater. He tossed the tube into the water and watched as the flames sputtered and the burning tube sank. Only then did he stop yelling, "Hot! Hot! Hot!"

He took off his gloves and wiped his forehead, like,

"Whew! That was a close one!" When he looked around to make sure that nobody had seen his weirdness, I ducked behind Lorena's curtain, so he didn't see me on his way back into his house.

Mom was right, I thought. *What an odd man.*

I couldn't see what was in the bushes that Garry had stuck his head into, but, whatever it was, he was talking to it.

"Let it go! Good boy! Let it go!"

And as he kept saying that, Garry was rocking back and forth on his knees like he was playing tug-of-war. Only he wasn't winning.

"Atta boy! Let it go! Who's a good boy?" he kept on.

Suddenly there was a thrashing in the underbrush, and Garry fell forward, crashing through branches onto his belly. Then Boing Boing burst from the hedge and ran straight at me with something in his mouth. I couldn't tell what it was until he dropped it at my feet, and then I *jumped.*

Because Boing Boing had brought me a foot. A human foot.

Only it wasn't attached to a human!! Where it should have been attached, there was only bone and blood and . . . oh, man! I don't think you want to hear this.

I gagged, "GAAAgggghhhh!"

Suddenly Garry was there, picking up the foot, like, *"Oh, yeah, I guess I dropped that."* When he straightened up, I could see that he was wearing the same rubber apron he had on the afternoon he drowned the flaming test tube. Only now, the front of the apron—you're not gonna believe this—was covered with *blood!*

I mean, it looked like blood.

I didn't know whether to hurl or scream or gag again. And before I made a choice, Garry spoke:

"Your dog . . . he, uh . . . he found . . . ," Garry stammered as he held up the foot. "And then he . . . uh, he . . ." And that's when *he chomped down on the foot!* It smooshed like a kitchen sponge.

I was about ready to pass out.

Garry released the foot from his teeth. "Then your dog . . . he . . ." Garry made little moves with his hands, like we were playing charades and he was trying to get me to say, *"ran away."*

It was while he was re-creating Boing Boing's kidnapping of the foot that Garry finally realized I was staring at it in his hand.

"Oh!" he yelped. "This . . . it's only . . . ," and, as he spoke, he squeezed the foot into a little ball and closed his hand around it. When he opened his fist, the foot sprang back into shape.

"See? Poof! Squishy." And he bit it again. "No pain!"

My head was throbbing with the realization of what a total wacko we had living next door.

Then Garry announced, "Okay!" turned and went back across the lawn and into his house, brushing grass and leaves and dirt off his rubber foot.

Now, maybe I have my little peculiarities.

And maybe I don't have any friends.

But, man, oh, man, I thought, *at least I'm not a nutjob like my neighbor Garry.*

6

I wasn't sure whether I should tell Mom the story about Garry and his squishy foot, but, by the time she got home that day, I had something else more important to tell her.

Something she wasn't going to like.

Mom had invited Vince to dinner that night. After all the times they had gone out together, it was the first time that Vince was coming to our house, so Mom asked me to cook something "special but not spicy."

And she asked Lorena to please be sure to be home. Mom didn't even say, "Be nice," or anything like that. Just, "Be here."

But while I was in the middle of dinner preparations, Lorena called and told me to tell Mom that Brad had offered her an extra shift at Chick-A-Dee, so she'd be eating at work and getting home after nine.

"I wish you'd told me before I defrosted this veal," I said as I minced my carrots and celery.

"Well, freeze it again," she snapped. Lorena doesn't understand how refreezing can damage meat.

"Maybe you should call Mom at work and tell her yourself," I suggested.

"I have a job to get to!" she yelled just before she hung up.

When Mom came in and I gave her Lorena's message, she froze. Then she nodded twice, which is always a dangerous sign. It means that she's trying to figure out just how mad she's going to get. It was so quiet in the kitchen that I could hear the gas flame under the water I was boiling for my wild rice.

Mom looked over all the stuff I had spread out on the countertops and on the stove, and she asked very quietly, "Need any help?"

"Nope. Everything's under control."

Mom nodded one more time, and she walked out, saying, "I'll go get ready, then."

Ooooh. She was *mad*.

If I hadn't hit Mom with Lorena's message as soon as she walked in, perhaps she would have asked me about the hairnet I was wearing.

I know. You're probably smacking your forehead and crying out, *"A hairnet? Why does a nine-year-old boy need to wear a hairnet?"*

I can explain.

On Monday morning that week everybody arrived at school to find that, over the weekend, someone had come in and put up public health posters. We were told it was because about three weeks before, a boy in the third grade had chipped a tooth trying to open a soda bottle with his teeth, so Principal Brandt had decided that safety was the most important issue in our young lives.

The posters warned us about dangers that lurked around every corner of our school building. For instance, one advised us that "SPEED LEADS TO SPILLS"; the poster showed a figure of a cartoon boy falling down stairs to his doom.

Another one showed kids slipping and sliding all over a freshly mopped hallway under the warning: "WHEN IT'S WET, DON'T GET WILD!"

You get the idea.

So, when I walked into the lunchroom at noon, I wasn't surprised to see a poster over the cafeteria line that announced: "KITCHEN STAFF MUST WEAR HAIRNETS AT ALL TIMES."

And, sure enough, that day, for the first time ever, all the ladies on the cafeteria line—and even Mr. Gorden, who works at the dishwashing machine and has hardly any hair—were wearing their nets.

And I thought, *That's a reasonable request.* Imagine all the germs that lurk on a strand of hair! I mean, nobody wants to find someone else's curls in their ice cream, do they?

So, since I knew that Mom was hoping this dinner for Vince would give him the best possible impression of our family, I decided that evening would provide the best opportunity for me to start my new cleanliness program.

I can understand that the hairnet might take some getting used to. And, perhaps, when Vince rang the doorbell at six-thirty and Mom called downstairs, *"Would you get that, honey?"* I should have given a little more thought to my appearance. But I was in the middle of chopping onions, and whenever I chop onions, I cry. I've tried all the tricks that I read about to prevent tears, but those darned onions always get to me.

I wiped my hands on a kitchen towel and opened the front door.

"Hey, Charley! How's it going?" Vincent boomed as he grabbed my hand and pumped it up and down. "Now, shake hands like I showed you. Squeeze my hand . . . ," and he squeezed mine, ". . . like you want to choke the life out of me! Squeeze it like you . . . huh?"

For the first time, he looked at me, and when he did, he stopped squeezing and pumping. Then he dropped my hand.

"Are you *crying?*"

"No," I sniffed, and wiped a tear off my cheek.

His face crinkled in disbelief. "Is that a hairnet?!" he gasped.

Behind me, Mom made her entrance.

"Well, this is a first! Dinner at home!"

Vince didn't say "hello" or tell Mom how nice she looked; instead, he pointed a finger at me and wagged it. "Why is he wearing a *hairnet?!*"

Mom stopped in her tracks and examined my head. I could see her eyes widen, but she struggled to keep her cool.

"I'm sure Charley has a good reason," she smiled.

I was back in the kitchen, standing on a chair and stirring my rice on a back burner, when I heard Mom and Vince whispering loudly in the living room. If I stopped stirring, I could pick out the highlights.

"That kid is always in the kitchen," Vince hissed.

"He likes to cook. And besides, I work late. Charley is a great help to me."

"But that's not normal," said Vince.

Mom's voice got louder. *"Are you saying my son isn't normal?"*

"I'm saying that a nine-year-old boy cooking and crying and wearing a hairnet is pretty . . . strange."

"Oh, so now he's 'strange'?"

"You know what I mean."

I could hear Mom's voice strain. *"No. What do you mean?"*

"I'm just thinking about people. People might see your kid and think that he's some kind of a . . . some kind of a . . ."

"Some kind of a what?" Mom pushed.

"Some kind of a . . . freak!"

I could tell from Mom's silence how upset Vince's words had made her. When she did speak, it was to say, *"Well. I'm sure you can find your way out."*

And she was right.

Later Mom and I sat quietly at the dining room table and pushed food around on our plates, because neither of us really felt like eating.

First of all, what Vince had said made me feel really awful.

Secondly, as much as I didn't like Vince, I guess my mom did. I felt kind of responsible for their fighting and for him stomping out and slamming the door, but I didn't know how to apologize for that.

Eventually Mom looked up with one of her brave smiles.

"So. Did you decide what you want to do for your birthday?" she asked.

I shrugged. "I don't need a party, if that's what you mean."

"No?" she wondered. "Won't your friends be disappointed?"

"Nah," I mumbled. "They have things to do."

"I'm sure they would change their plans. What if I call their mothers and . . . ?"

"Mom," I stopped her. I put my hand on hers, hoping that I could soften the blow of what I was about to say. "I don't really have any friends."

She gazed at me for a while, and I got the feeling that I wasn't telling her anything she didn't know.

"Well. Maybe a party is a good way to make some."

I think she had it backwards: I think you've got to make friends, and *then* you can invite them to a party. Either way, my party wasn't going to happen. But I could tell that it mattered a lot to Mom, so I decided that I would disappoint her slowly.

"Can I let you know?" I lied.

She nodded, and took a forkful of dinner.

"Mmmm," she hummed as she chewed. "Your sister doesn't know what she's missing. It's beef stew, right?"

"Actually," I said, "it's veal osso buco with shallots in a red wine reduction."

"Oh," Mom nodded carefully. "Of course."

It's times like that when I bet she's wondering: *Was there some mix-up at the hospital? Instead of my own baby boy, did they hand me an alien life-form?*

But I smiled at Mom.

She smiled back.

And then we finished everything on our plates.

7

That night, when Lorena finally got home, Mom unloaded on her for missing dinner, so I decided that would be a good time to take Boing Boing for a long walk.

As we roamed the street, I made some important decisions.

#1. The hairnet had to go.

#2. I was not a freak.

#3. I had to tell Mom that I didn't want a birthday party; once we got past that, we could figure out some other way to celebrate my "big day."

And then something happened that changed my life forever.

I'm not kidding.

I was deep in thought, and Boing Boing was sniffing around one of Mrs. Cleveland's big trees when I heard loud voices. And they weren't coming from my house.

Suddenly the door to Crazy Garry's house *flew* open and his girlfriend Pincushion rushed out, followed by Garry. They couldn't see Boing Boing and me watching from the shadows across the street.

Pincushion stomped down the driveway, carrying a cardboard box and a big suitcase. Garry chased after her, pleading, "Don't go! *Please!*"

As Pincushion flung her stuff into the backseat of her convertible, she shouted, "I can't take this anymore, Garry. I can't! You're too weird."

And I thought: *Isn't that what I've been saying all along?*

Garry pleaded, "So I'll . . . I'll change! I'll need instructions, but *I can change.*"

Pincushion scoffed, "You can't change, Garry. Look at you. You're a grown man with no social skills . . ."

You tell him, lady!

". . . no fashion sense . . ."

Amen!

". . . and no friends!"

Whoa, lady! Now you've crossed the line.

I must have gasped, because Boing Boing stopped his sniffing and looked up at me. After all, Pincushion had come awfully close to describing *me*, and COME ON! No matter what could be said about me, I was not like Garry.

Was I?

Pincushion jumped into her car, started it, and then—as if she'd read my mind and understood my deepest fear—she whipped around to Garry and, before she peeled out of the driveway, she spit out, "Face it, Garry. You're a *freak!*"

I felt the earth drop away from under me. *That word!* Twice in one night. One word—the *same* word!—used to describe me and the *weirdest guy on the planet!*

As Pincushion careened out of the driveway, she crashed through some of the bushes that separate our property from Garry's. She spun the wheel and as she turned, her headlights raked across Mrs. Cleveland's front lawn.

That's when Garry saw me.

As Pincushion roared away, Garry and I stood there for one horrible moment, looking sadly across the street at each other.

Two friendless freaks.

And then I started to run.

With Boing Boing nipping at my heels, I ran faster than I have ever run. Across our lawn! Up on our porch! I blasted through our front door as if the Goblins of GlugGlug (*Monsters & Maniacs,* Issue 25) were at my back.

"Mom! Mom!" I ran from room to room, yelling my head off.

Mom rushed out of the laundry room, carrying a basket of clothes. "What, Charley? What?"

Lorena raced down from upstairs shouting, "He'd better be bleeding!"

I was practically wailing by this time: "MaaaaaaaaaahhM!"

Mom dropped her basket of laundry, fell to her knees and grabbed me by both shoulders.

"I'm right here, Charley!" she shouted. "What is it?"

I gulped a big ball of air, and I said it.

Yup. I actually said it.

"I gotta have a birthday party."

8

That night in bed, there were about a hundred thoughts running around in my brain, all trying to get my attention. And one thought kept poking at the top of my skull. One thought kept shouting louder than all the rest.

And that one thought was this: *I'm going to have a birthday party.*

Me.

Charley Maplewood.

I'm going to invite kids to my party.

And they will come.

Why?

Because, I told myself, *I am going to throw the best party— in the history—OF THE WORLD!*

And as I thought that, I thrust my fists above my head in triumph. Unfortunately, there's a wall there, so I cracked my knuckles pretty hard and made a loud BOOM! that caused Mom to poke her head in and say, "Are you okay?"

"Yeah," I answered. "Yeah. I'm great."

THE
BIRTHDAY NOTEBOOK

9

As I raced around getting ready for school the next morning, it hit me that I had a lot of work ahead. After all, with my birthday less than three weeks away, I had to get organized. I decided that the best way to keep all my ideas in order was to put them all in one place.

I have a super-special spiral notebook: my *Monsters & Maniacs* Official Record. In it I list every story in every issue, and after each entry I write a short description about the story and the characters in it. Then, using a rating system that I created, I give each story one, two, three or four daggers, four being the best rating a story can get.

I decided on rating with daggers because they're actually pretty easy to draw.

But all of my *Monsters & Maniacs* stuff only takes up about half the notebook, so, while Mom yelled from downstairs, "You're gonna be late!" I opened to the middle of the book, and across the top of the page I wrote: THINGS TO DO FOR MY PARTY. Down the left side of the page, I numbered the lines from 1 to 10.

I didn't have anything to write on any of the lines yet, but it felt good to get started.

On our way out to the car, Mom saw our mangled bushes. She stopped suddenly and gasped, "Now what in the *world?!*"

I guess that, in the excitement of my previous night's announcement, I had completely forgotten to tell her how Pincushion had driven her car through our hedge. So when Mom looked to me and shook her head in confusion and dismay, I just shrugged and shook my head, too.

Before the first bell that day, I sat way off at one end of the playground and studied my Birthday Notebook.

THINGS TO DO FOR MY PARTY was all I had written so far.

But on my way to school that morning, I kept rerunning the memory of Pincushion's screeching departure from Garry's house the night before. And when I remembered how she had yelled, *"You have no friends!"* I realized what belonged on line 1. So I wrote it in:

1. MAKE FRIENDS

I stared at those words. *How?* I wondered. *How how how how?* And then it hit me!

So I wrote on line 2 . . .

2. WATCH PEOPLE WITH FRIENDS TO LEARN HOW

. . . but as I finished, Jennifer suddenly shoved an issue of *Monsters & Maniacs* between my face and my Birthday Plan.

"Check it out!" she said. "I went through this issue and counted every time they use the word 'booger' and the word 'barf,' and which one do you think won?"

I looked up at her. I could tell that Jennifer had eaten an apple for breakfast, because bits of its red skin were still in her braces. I didn't answer, hoping that she would realize she had interrupted something very important and leave me alone. After a long pause she shrugged, still smiling.

"Okay. Think about it. Tell me later. I'll just go stand over . . . there."

She pointed to a patch of dead grass about twenty feet away.

"It's a free country," was all I said.

At lunch, I got my first chance to watch friendship at work.

Across the room, I saw Donna eating with Dina and Dana. Just as they finished their lunches, Donna reached into her shoulder bag and, with a little *ta-da!* move, pulled out two new unsharpened pencils. They were thick and pink and, from the end where the eraser should be, little colorful yarn balls dangled.

Donna presented one to Dina and one to Dana, and you would have thought that the two of them had just won a Jeep or something, the way they squealed and clapped and hugged Donna.

I opened my Birthday Notebook and, under WATCH PEO-PLE WITH FRIENDS TO LEARN HOW, I wrote: *You can buy friends with gifts.*

I was excited to have discovered such an important fact, until I dug into my pocket and pulled out all the money I had.

A nickel and a dime. Fifteen cents. That wasn't going to buy too many friends.

But there must be other ways to make friends, because not everybody has tons of money. I decided I needed to find one of those inexpensive ways.

❋   ❋   ❋

That afternoon, I was at my locker when our Class President Leo hobbled by on crutches.

Oh, didn't I tell you? The big news in school that morning was that Leo broke his foot.

From what I overheard in the halls and the classrooms, I was able to piece together the story: the previous afternoon, Leo was messing around with a bunch of guys, and he had jumped off the roof of his house. Everybody was saying how he had done it "millions of times before," but this time he "landed wrong," and all the guys who were there heard a "loud crunch."

Ouch. The word "crunch" made me wince each time I overheard it.

So today Leo showed up on crutches with his foot in a white cast, which everybody started writing on so that, by lunchtime, it was covered with people's signatures and drawings of lightning bolts.

Because Leo had to hold on to the crutches to walk, a bunch of guys were following him around—carrying his books, carrying his lunch tray, opening his locker and stuff. And they all kept asking Leo how he felt and patting him on his shoulder and saying how sorry they were.

And I thought: *Wow.*

I opened my Birthday Notebook and under *You can buy friends with gifts,* I wrote *You can get friends with sympathy.*

But later that afternoon, when I stood on the high brick wall at the far end of the school parking lot and looked down on the hard, black asphalt where I was planning to "land wrong" and suffer a minor injury—an injury that would attract my very own mob of friends—I had second thoughts.

Isn't there some way, I wondered, to get friends without getting hurt and requiring medical attention?

I decided to keep looking.

As I was climbing down off the wall, I *did* scrape my elbow kinda badly, but I didn't think that I could win any sympathy with a big scab, so I never showed it to anyone.

A few days later as I skateboarded home, I stopped to watch a baseball game in the playground, and, as I looked on from the sidelines, something amazing happened.

A baseball player raced from third plate and slid home in a cloud of dust. Well, the reaction he got was *incredible!* His teammates went berserk, pounding him on the back, patting him on the head and screaming things like, "Way to go, pal!" and "That was awesome, buddy!"

"Pal"?

"Buddy"?

Aha!

I opened my Birthday Notebook and, underneath *You can get friends with sympathy,* I began to write *Sports heroes make tons of friends.*

But I never got to finish.

That's because the very next batter popped up a ball that flew out of bounds in a high arc and fell—BOINK!—right down on my head! The sudden and surprising impact made me drop my Birthday Notebook and sit down, stunned, right where I had been standing.

I rubbed my head, where a lump was starting to form.

None of the ballplayers made a move toward me. The school groundskeeper, Mr. Gavin, came over, knelt down and held two fingers up in front of my face.

"How many fingers?" he asked. When I answered correctly, he told me to go home and put ice on my bump, which was starting to hurt something fierce.

But not as much as it hurt to hear the ballplayers' snorts and titters as I staggered away from the playground.

So much for being a sports hero.

I was going to erase that one from my Birthday Notebook. As a matter of fact, I vowed to go home and scratch out *You can get friends with sympathy*, too.

But before I could go home, I still had to go shopping for that night's dinner.

And that's when things got real strange.

10

As I walked the aisles of the Happy Giant Supermarket, my head kept throbbing where that baseball had crashed down on me.

But then I turned my cart into the bakery aisle.

Normally, I would roll right past that section of the store, because Mom and Lorena don't eat a lot of desserts. But that day I slowed down and looked up, up, up at the shelves and shelves of cake mixes and cans of frosting that rose high above me. And in that moment, staring up at that Great Wall of Cake, my head stopped hurting and the discouraging thoughts of my unsuccessful hunt for a friend flew from my mind. One thought and one thought alone remained: *"I'm going to have a birthday party,"* I told myself, *"so I will need a birthday cake."*

But what kind? Chocolate? Dark Swiss Chocolate? Angel Food? Devil's Food? Lemon Mousse? Butterscotch Swirl? So many choices!

I pulled a box of Confetti Coconut Cake Mix off the shelf to look over the directions. I had just started reading: "In a large bowl, combine . . . ," when the box was smacked upward, out of my hands, and a familiar voice whined, *"Ooooh! Who's gonna bake a cake?"*

It was Cougar. And, of course, Scottie was right behind him. What they were doing in the store was probably illegal, but there they were.

I yelled, "Cougar! Scottie! Stop it!"

As the box fell from the air, Cougar snatched it and tossed it over my head to Scottie, who bleated, "*Charley's* gonna bake a cake!"

"C'mon, give it back!" I said as they played keep-away with my cake mix.

I really should have known better, because they started to mimic my words, but in high, screechy voices: "C'mon! Give it back! Give it back!"

I finally grabbed the box at the same moment Scottie caught it. Then Cougar seized it, too, and the three of us wrestled for control while they continued to rag on me.

"You wear an apron when you cook?"

"I bet he's got a really cute apron!"

"STOP IT!" I yelled, and I yanked at the box.

And it exploded.

Confetti Coconut Cake Mix flew up in the air and covered everything with a fine, white powder.

We all stopped and looked at each other. What had we done? We destroyed a box of cake mix that we *hadn't even paid for!*

Cougar and Scottie suddenly heaved with laughter, stepped back from the scene of devastation and pointed at *me!*

"CLEANUP ON AISLE THREE!" Cougar yelled so the whole store could hear.

I wailed, "I didn't do it! I didn't do it!" but who was I kidding? I was holding the box. I was covered with powder. And it was their word against mine.

So I dropped the box and pushed my cart up to speeds that its little wheels were hardly designed for. I skidded around corners and veered around shoppers as Scottie and Cougar chased me, chanting, "Cleanup on aisle three! Cleanup on aisle three!"

But then I turned down an aisle and found that—oh, no!—I was headed straight for a cart that was blocking the aisle sideways! I couldn't stop in time, and I smashed right into it.

Everything got quiet. And I immediately noticed something weird: the cart was filled to the top with about fifty bags of potato chips. And nothing else.

And the worst part?

That cart belonged to Garry Quarky, my neighbor. The freak.

He looked up. I looked up. He blinked when he recognized me.

"Oh," he said, pointing at me. "You're . . ." And then he stopped, because he didn't know my name. So he simply said, ". . . you."

I was so stunned that it took me a moment to remember I was being chased. I glanced back and there, ten paces behind me, Cougar and Scottie waited, smirking.

Garry cleared his throat. "Shopping," he said. He pointed to his cart and explained, "Yup. That's what I'm doing. Doing the shopping."

He really talked like that.

I would gladly have left him at that moment, but I couldn't. His cart still blocked the aisle, and I sure wasn't going to turn around and get dragged by Cougar and Scottie back to the scene of our crime in aisle three. My thoughts were interrupted when Garry started stammering, "See, my girl . . . girlfr . . . girlfriend . . . y'know? Stacy?"

Stacy? I thought; Pincushion's name was really *Stacy?*

"She . . . uh, Stacy used to shop. But now she's . . ." and he flapped his hands like a bird winging off.

"She's gone," I suggested.

"Yeah," he mumbled, and his voice cracked a little. He sniffed and dabbed what might have been a tear from his eye, and the little voice inside my head was screaming: *"Oh, man! Is he crying? Please don't let him cry in the supermarket! Not in front of* Cougar and Scottie!*"*

But Garry wiped his nose, cleared his throat, and then, like he had just awakened from a terrible spell that had turned him temporarily stupid, he asked me in a clear, adult voice, "Can I ask you *one* thing?"

I was so startled by the change in his tone that I simply nodded.

Garry pointed at his cart full of fifty bags of potato chips and asked, "Is this enough?"

"For . . . ?"

"For . . . now? Is this enough *for now?*"

I tried to puzzle out what he was asking: *Are you wondering if fifty bags of potato chips are enough to keep you alive for a while?* But then that leads to the question: *Are potato chips all you plan to eat?*

He must have sensed the wheels whirring in my head, because he pointed at my cart and explained, "I mean, look at you. You. You really *shop.* You got your chicken . . . parts. Got your, uh . . . green vegetable . . ."

"Broccoli," I offered.

"Right. Broccoli. Full of iron. Vitamin C. Good stuff, broccoli. Right?" He looked up and saw that I was staring at him strangely; he immediately dropped his head and turned his cart away.

"Y'know what? I've bothered you enough. 'Kay. Bye."

And off he went. Leaving me at the mercy of Cougar and Scottie, who I could feel creeping up behind me. So I did something that I could never have imagined myself ever, ever doing in a million years.

I called after Garry.

"Where's your protein?"

He stopped, turned around and squinted.

"Huh?"

"You really should have protein in every meal. Potato chips are not protein."

I looked back at Cougar and Scottie. They were bored. Cougar nudged Scottie with a "C'mon," and they were gone.

Behind me, Garry protested, "But I don't cook."

I turned back to him. "Can you reach the sink?" I asked.

He nodded a slow "Yes."

"Then you can cook."

11

Trying to explain cooking to Garry Quarky was like trying to explain a computer to a cat. Garry didn't understand how to peel vegetables, or why you simmer soups, or how to broil a hamburger. Heck, he didn't know the difference between lettuce and cabbage.

Finally, after we cruised a bunch of aisles without adding anything to Garry's cart, he turned to me.

"Where's the stuff in boxes?"

And don't ask me how, but I knew what he was talking about.

We stood before the big frozen TV dinners cases, and I thought Garry was going to cry again. One by one, he took boxes out of the cold and lovingly touched the pictures on the covers: photos of fried chicken and meat loaf and beef pot pies that looked just like the meal waiting for Garry inside the cardboard.

Garry put thirty-six TV dinners in his cart, and he would have taken more, but I told him that that was "enough." For now.

I got the rest of my groceries, and then Garry followed me to the checkout lines, where he rolled his cart up right behind mine. There were a few large carts ahead of us, so we waited in silence until I finally got up the courage to say:

"Now can I ask *you* one thing?"

"Sure," he nodded.

I took deep breath, not sure how he was going to handle my question. "Okay. Here goes. Remember that day you chased Boing Boing into the hedge cuz he stole something of yours?"

Garry looked confused. " 'Boing Boing'?"

"My dog. His name's Boing Boing," I explained.

"Oh," he nodded. "So that's the noise you're making when you're running around? I thought it was some kind of game you play. With an imaginary friend."

An imaginary friend? Whoa! I thought. *How old do you think I am?*

"No. Just my dog," I assured Garry. "Anyway, that day you were in the hedge on your knees? In your rubber apron, remember? And Boing Boing was chewing on something and . . . ?"

"Oh, yeah. Right, right."

As we spoke, a lady wearing a lot of lipstick and biting her fingernails rolled her cart behind Garry.

I continued to him: "What was that . . . *thing*?"

"Well, what did it look like?"

I shrugged: "It looked like you had chopped off some-body's foot or something . . ."

The lady behind Garry snapped her head up as I added: ". . . like you hacked it off at the ankle."

"Exactly!" Garry exclaimed. "That's what I was going for!"

The lady's eyes opened wide.

"And was that blood? Cuz it looked like it was dripping with blood," I wondered.

"Yes!" Garry cried. "But did you think that there was too much blood? I always worry that there's too much blood."

That's when the lady made a little *"Yeep!"* sound and raced away so quickly that her shopping cart left skid marks on the tile floor. Garry and I both looked after her. Then we shrugged at each other.

Suddenly, out of nowhere, he said, "My name is Garry."

"I know. *Garry Quarky.*"

He seemed surprised that I knew both his names, so I added: "Sometimes your mail comes to us by mistake, so . . ."

"Ah," he nodded. "I don't know yours. Your name."

"Oh. I'm Charley. Charley Maplewood."

He extended a hand, so I shook it, but I didn't squeeze it as hard as Vince had been trying to get me to.

There was a little awkward pause until I asked: "Okay. So. This foot-thing? What's that about?"

"Well, Charley," said Garry, "I'll show you."

12

Garry Quarky's garage was amazing.

Where ordinary people would park their car, Garry had built this . . . this *laboratory*, a wacky workshop full of unbelievable objects and machines and drawings and other nifty things. When he first snapped on the overhead lights, I couldn't stop saying "Wow!" for about ten minutes.

He had little models of spaceships, but spaceships like you've never seen. Some of them looked like pirate ships with rocket thrusters coming out the back, and others looked like fish with steel wings. A bunch of them hung from wires overhead, dangling up there next to miniature planets with rings and stars and volcanoes shooting off of them.

Garry had hundreds of clay models of dinosaurs—some of which actually lived a million years ago, and others that he just made up.

He had created monsters that have, like, twelve arms, seven legs, horns instead of eyes, and hair made out of snakes.

And then there were the body parts.

There were phony noses and ears thumbtacked up on Garry's bulletin board; there were rubber fingers and hands and toes and feet scattered all over. And eyeballs! Everywhere I looked, Garry's rubber eyeballs looked back at me, all squishy and soft. Most of them were a dull gray color, but some of them were painted to look like the real thing.

Garry even had complete faces lying around, sort of like Halloween masks, but *much* realer. They were the faces of actual people who all volunteered to let Garry slather some kind of goo all over their faces and make masks of them. I don't know who those people were, but if I saw them again on the street I would recognize them immediately!

"I used to do this," Garry said, after I finally stopped gasping and gawking at everything in the workroom.

"Do '*this*'?" I asked. "You mean, make fakes?"

"They're called 'effects,' " Garry corrected me. "I did 'effects.' "

"Whoa," I marveled, still looking around. "For what?"

"For movies."

"For Hollywood?"

"Not Hollywood," he shook his head. "North Carolina. Believe it or not, they make movies there, too."

"In North Carolina? Really?"

"Really," Garry smiled, looking around, and from the way he spoke, I got the feeling like North Carolina must have been a special time in his life.

"So how come you're in Fresno now?" I asked.

Garry's face sagged, like the air had gone out of his cheeks, and he looked away from me as he sighed, "I . . . I stopped."

There was a silence then, and I could only hear the hum of the fluorescent bulbs on the ceiling. I decided not to ask him any more about North Carolina that day.

"So, tell me about the noses," I said, pointing to about thirty different sizes and shapes that were lined up along a workbench like little soldiers.

That question seemed to perk Garry right up. "Oh! Noses. Now, noses are fun."

"Why?"

"Because! I can take a cast of anybody's nose, and by adding a bump here or a wart there, I can turn that person into a wizard or a monster or whatever I choose. The possibilities . . . they're endless!"

Excitedly, he crossed to a bulletin board from which he pulled a thumbtacked ear. "Ears, on the other hand, ears can be difficult. They're full of crevices and corners, and it can be really hard to . . . ."

He suddenly stopped and turned to me.

"Is this boring?"

"No!" I almost yelled. "How can you ask that?"

"Well. Cuz Stacy, my girlfriend . . ." then he corrected himself: "my *ex*-girlfriend . . . she was always telling me how boring I can be."

"No," I assured him.

He crinkled up his nose. "Really?"

"Really." I gestured around the room. "Just look at this— it's awesome! The spaceships and the creatures and the squishy feet—we could talk about this stuff for hours, and I would *never* get bored."

So that's just what we did.

13

When I ran into the kitchen late that afternoon and started telling Mom about my afternoon at Garry's, I found her rushing around, putting ice in glasses, pouring peanuts into a bowl, and straightening her hair a lot.

"And all those things—the models and dinosaurs and noses and stuff—he calls them *effects*, y'know? But he doesn't do *effects* anymore, on account of something that happened in North Carolina that he doesn't really want to talk about."

"Doesn't want to talk about," Mom muttered absentmindedly.

"So now, he has a new business and he works out of his house . . . see?"

I held up the business card that Garry had given me when I left his house. Above the words GARRY QUARKY: THE IDEA MAN was a little drawing of a glowing lightbulb.

"Look! It says right here: he's 'the Idea Man.' Pretty cool, right?"

"Very cool," Mom smiled, never slowing down. At that moment I could have told her that I was going to shave my head and join a motorcycle gang, and she would have answered, "Very cool."

Mom turned and blinked at me, as if she was surprised to find that she wasn't alone in the kitchen.

"Oh! Hi, honey," she smiled. "Where are the cheese crackers?"

She knows where the cheese crackers are, but I could tell that her brain was off about a mile away, so I pointed to the cupboard. Then I continued.

"And what that means—being 'the Idea Man'—is that companies from all over the world call him and pay him to come up with ideas to make their businesses run better and stuff. He's *that* smart, Mom."

"Smart. Wow," she answered in her blurry way. "And who is this?" She picked up a tray with snacks and cold drinks on it and headed out of the kitchen.

"Garry," I said.

"Is he a new teacher?"

"No! Garry! Next-door-Garry!"

Mom stopped in her tracks and turned to me.

"That creepy man? Why on earth are you talking to him?"

And that's when I stopped and gasped. "Well, why are you talking to *him*?"

I pointed across the room to where Vince was sitting on the sofa.

I thought that the whole Mom-and-Vince thing had ended the night he called me a *freak* and slammed out of our house. But I guess he had been phoning her at work and apologizing, and that must have worked, because here he was on the couch, like a stain you can't get rid of.

"Hey, Killer," Vince smiled and stuck his hand out. "How about a handshake?"

I didn't move.

"Charley, honey?" Mom chirped. "Vince and I have been talking, and he feels . . . he feels really . . . really . . ."

"Bad," Vince helped her out. "I feel bad about missing that dinner you cooked the other night."

"And Vince has something that he wants to contribute to your birthday party," Mom added quickly. "Tell him, sweetie."

Sweetie? She called Vince *sweetie?*

Vince sat forward and cleared his throat. "Well, yeah. Down at my store, The Paradise Pantry, I kind of run the show." He looked to Mom. "Who'm I kidding? I *do* run the show!" Then they both laughed.

I didn't.

"So," Vince continued, "when you figure out what you want to do about a birthday cake for this big wingding of yours, you come to me, and I'll fix you up. Whaddya say?"

I didn't say anything.

But Vince looked to Mom with a look that said, *"How was that?"*

And instead of nodding or winking at him, Mom leaned over and *gave him a kiss!* It wasn't a long one; more like a little peck.

But, still! *A kiss!!*

"I can make my own cake," I said in a very low voice, hoping to show Vince who was boss around here.

"I'm sure you can, buddy," he chuckled, "but can you decorate it? Cuz I've got a crew down there in the bakery department who can give you a birthday cake that'll blow the top of your head off. And you know what I've been thinking of for you? Do you?" He leaned forward and whispered: *"Cowboys."*

I twitched. "What about them?"

"As a theme. For your party."

Are you kidding me?! I thought. *Maybe you haven't heard about Jamie Wiggerty's birthday party? About me and the pony? Maybe you didn't have to put up with the whispers that went on for years afterward, the snickers in school hallways of, "Giddyap, Cowboy!" But I can tell you right here and now that there is no way I will allow anything even remotely "cowboy-like" to ruin my birthday party!*

I didn't say any of that, of course. I only thought it as I stood there, listening, while Vince enjoyed the sound of his own voice.

"Yeah, we do a swell Cowboy Cake," he boasted. "Little plastic horses. Little cows in little corrals. And we got these teeny-weeny cactuses."

"Cacti," I corrected him.

"Huh?"

" 'Cacti.' It's the plural of 'cactus.' "

"Oh. Whatever. You come to me once you've got a theme." Vince looked me in the eye. "You *are* gonna have a theme, aren't you?"

A *theme?!*

Nobody had ever told me I would need a theme!

I trudged up to my bedroom and opened my Birthday Notebook to the heading: THINGS TO DO FOR MY PARTY.

Below that, #1 and #2 still stared back at me: MAKE FRIENDS and WATCH PEOPLE WITH FRIENDS TO LEARN HOW. I groaned.

I hadn't done either one of those yet, and now, suddenly, I had an entirely new, additional duty.

Underneath them I wrote: #3. GET A THEME, and it felt like the weight of the world had just dropped onto my shoulders.

14

As I passed by in the school hallway the next day, I overheard Donna telling Dina and Dana about a party that she had been to recently. Ordinarily I wouldn't have been interested, but when she said, "And guess what the theme was!" I flattened myself against a locker around the corner to listen for any suggestions I could pick up.

"*Princesses.* It was an all-princesses birthday!" Donna exclaimed.

She went on and on about how all the girls at the party got their hair piled up on top of their heads, and then they put on fake jewel crowns and they ate little sandwiches with the crusts cut off. From the way that Dana and Dina were squealing and gasping, I guess that teensy sandwiches are somebody's idea of a good time, but no.

No cowboys.

No princesses.

No, thank you.

Later, in the upstairs boys' room, I asked Darryl Egbert if he'd ever had a birthday party. I thought it would be a good time to ask; he had just gotten a 100 on a science quiz, so I figured he wouldn't be throwing up anytime soon.

"A birthday party? As a matter of fact, yes. Once," Darryl nodded carefully. "I was turning eight. I was allowed to invite four friends from the Pre-Teen Chess Club to join me for the occasion."

"The Chess Club? So was that the theme of the party?" I asked eagerly.

"What are you talking about?"

"The *theme*. Was 'chess' your theme? Did you dress up like kings and rooks and knights? And was your cake decorated like a checkerboard?"

Darryl regarded me strangely. "*No*. Actually, my father drove the five of us up to San Francisco. To Chinatown."

I had been to Chinatown, so I knew about the cool shops and restaurants and banners and paper dragons everywhere.

"Oh, okay, so was *Chinatown* your theme?" I asked. "Did you have Chinese food? And did you light Chinese sparklers instead of candles on your cake?"

"No!" Darryl was getting annoyed now. "My father knows a very inexpensive barber in Chinatown. So we all got haircuts. And afterward, on the way home, we ate sandwiches my mother had packed."

Darryl smiled at the memory. "Yeah. That was fun," he said, and then he walked out.

"I had a Backstage Birthday. That's a good theme, don't you think?"

I hadn't even asked Jennifer Mobley for suggestions, but there she was, cornering me in the library after school. I had gone in there hoping to find books on "birthdays" and "themes," but before I could look them up in the card catalogue, Jennifer dragged me into an empty aisle.

She had heard from Darryl about how I had "bombarded" him with "very odd questions" about "birthday themes and Chinese food."

"So! I was gonna be seven," she began in her annoying voice, "and my mom noticed that a tour of *The Lion King* stage show was coming to the Saroyan Theatre downtown, y'know? So, because she knows I really, *really* love music and dancing and singing, she got tickets for me and eleven of my friends to go. It was going to be so great!"

She held up a finger for each part of her story: "*First*, we were going to see the show; *second*, we were all going to get souvenir T-shirts; *third*, we were going to go backstage and meet one of the dancers who played a leopard or a parrot or something. And finally . . . !"

Jennifer smiled real wide and shook her red curls out. "Finally, we were going to have birthday cake that had, like, a theater stage drawn on it, with the curtains parting and a picture of me in the frosting, like I was walking out into the spotlight! It was so beautiful!"

She sighed.

"It's such a shame that we never got to do any of that."

"Why?"

"All because of Jeffrey Stovall."

"Why? What did Jeffrey Stovall do?" I wondered.

"Well, everybody was having a good time, up until the scene when Simba watches his father get trampled to death by the water buffaloes. That part is so sad, don't you think?"

I shrugged. "I guess."

"When that scene happened, Jeffrey Stovall started sobbing. Not just crying. *Sobbing.* Then it was like a flu that gets passed around; one by one, each of my friends started weeping. And they wouldn't stop!

"At intermission, Mom decided we should leave, and I couldn't talk her out of it. So when we all climbed into the van without seeing the second act or getting the T-shirts or going backstage, I couldn't help myself; *I* started to cry.

"And when my mom pulled onto the freeway, things got even worse. She was in such a hurry that she zoomed past a policeman on a motorcycle, so he flipped on his siren and came after us. And when my mom saw his flashing lights and had to pull over, even *she* started to cry.

"So, now my friends were wailing and sobbing, 'What did we do wrong?' I was still pretty upset about missing Act II of *The Lion King,* so I told them that we were all going to jail because we left the theater early.

"That made them wail even louder.

"Then, as my mom was handing over her driver's license to the cop, Jeffrey Stovall had his accident."

"What accident?" I couldn't believe that Jennifer had tricked me into caring about how her story ended.

"Well, after crying for so long, Jeffrey had a headache and a stomachache, so that's why he leaned out his window and threw up onto the policeman's boots."

"*No!*"

Jennifer nodded.

"And unfortunately, Jeffrey's vomiting had the same effect on all of us that his crying had in the theater."

"You don't mean . . ."

"Uh-hunh. Everybody started puking right and left. When the policeman saw all these kids blowing chunks—and even though he had Jeffrey Stovall's breakfast all over his boots—he took pity on my mom. He got on his motorcycle and turned on his siren and gave us a police escort home."

"A police escort? Really?" I was impressed.

"Yeah. That part was cool, but by then, nobody had an appetite, so we never lit the candles or cut my cake or anything. And when everybody's parents came to pick them up, they were all still crying, so their parents stared at my mom and wondered what she had done to upset their children so terribly.

"Plus, the van smelled for about a year afterward, even after Mom and Dad scrubbed it out with bleach about seven times. So. That was my Backstage Birthday."

Jennifer sighed real deep and her eyes got a dreamy look in them.

"I'll never forget a single minute of it."

Then she snapped her head around to me. "Why were you asking?"

"Huh? Oh!" I stammered. "No reason."

15

After school, I sat on the bank of the drainage canal behind the school, stared at my Birthday Notebook and shook my head. Time was slipping away. My "big day" was approaching fast, and I hadn't done *anything* on my THINGS TO DO FOR MY BIRTHDAY list. I was desperate.

How desperate? I'll tell you how desperate.

I went to ask my sister for advice.

"What're you asking me for?" Lorena scowled when I pushed ahead of a long line of people waiting at her cash register in the Chick-A-Dee Restaurant. I figured that it was okay for me to cut in line because I didn't want food. Just a theme.

"*Because.* If I don't get a theme of my own, Mom and Vince are going to make me have a cowboy birthday party."

"Ugh," Lorena groaned. "Cowboys are so lame. QUIT IT!"

She didn't say that last thing to me; that was for Brad, her supervisor, who had come up behind her and pinched her fanny. As usual, Brad was wearing his "talk-to-me-People!" headset in a special way so that it wouldn't muss his hair, which he spends about ten hours arranging every day.

"What? My hand slipped," Brad grinned as he slid a tray toward the guy at the head of the line. "Three pieces white meat. Large fries," Brad smiled. "Thanks for eating at Chick-A-Dee."

Then he winked at Lorena and went back into the kitchen, barking into his headset, "People! Where are my onion rings?"

Lorena rolled her eyes. "He's always grabbing my butt."

"In *Monsters & Maniacs*, y'know, the July issue? This girl sticks a fork in a guy's hand for doing that," I advised.

Behind me, a lady with a big red purse whined, "Can I order, miss?"

"Charley, beat it," snapped Lorena. "I gotta work."

"But what about my theme? For my party? I need a theme!"

"Well, don't come crying to me! I don't have any ideas. You need somebody with ideas."

And I swear my jaw dropped open. That was one of the few times in her whole life that Lorena actually said something that made sense.

Because I *did* know somebody with ideas.

"Actually, I'm what people call a consultant," Garry explained.

"But your card says 'the Idea Man.' Is that really you or did you just buy cards that said that already?" I asked.

"Well, I have ideas, sure. But they're . . . they're for businesses."

"But you agree, don't you? There's no way I can do a cowboy theme for my birthday party."

"No," Garry shook his head. "Cowboys . . . cowboys are really tired."

"Thank you!" I yelled.

I looked around at the room we were in. Garry had emptied one of the bedrooms in his house and made an office where he goes to work every morning. It's filled with computers and copy machines and stacks of files and piles of papers. There's a map with little colored pins pushed into cities all over the United States and Asia and Europe, and above that, six different wall clocks are set to the time in Tokyo, Honolulu, Los Angeles, New York, London and Rome.

"You work in here all day?" I asked.

"All day."

"And in your garage all night?"

"Uh-huh. Want something to drink?" Garry led me into the kitchen, where empty TV dinner boxes were scattered all over the countertops.

"Love those TV dinners, huh?" I said.

"Oh. Yeah." He picked up a few of the boxes, embarrassed that the place was such a mess.

I sat on a high stool at his kitchen counter. "Okay. I won't take up much more of your time, but I need a theme for my party. Fast."

As he poured glasses of water, Garry shook his head. "No no no. You don't want to rush this."

"But I gotta! My birthday is only a few weeks away."

"Ah. But!" He turned to me. "This is no ordinary birthday, huh? This is a big one." He held up one finger. "The big one . . . ," and, with the other hand, he made a circle, ". . . oh. The Big One-Oh. Get it?"

I stared at his finger figures for few seconds until I realized what he was making with his fingers. "Ten!" I cried.

"*One-Oh*. Yeah. I'm gonna be ten."

Garry nodded. "Double digits, huh? Life begins."

The way he said that flooded me with such a feeling of specialness. A feeling of importance. A feeling of . . .

"Now, how in the world did that get there?" Garry suddenly said, squinting at something on the finger he used to make the "one."

"What?" I said, leaning forward to see.

"Oh, it's just this fingernail. It's . . . it's longer than it should be." And, as he said that, Garry laid his finger down on a chopping block, picked up a big kitchen knife, and WHAM!, brought it down and *chopped off his finger!*

I just about flew backward off my kitchen stool before I realized that there wasn't any blood. As a matter of fact, the knife just kind of bounced off the rubber finger that Garry had substituted at the last minute.

"Didn't scare you, huh?"

I shook my head. "Sorta. Not really."

"Well, dang," he sighed. "It's something that I've been working on." Then he held up the squishy finger for me to see.

"I think it needs work."

He nodded in agreement. I reached out and took the phony finger from him. "These are so cool." I looked up at him. "How do you make them?"

"Oh, it's easy. Did you ever make a footprint in wet concrete?"

"Once," I nodded. "When we poured a new patio at our old house."

"Okay. So now imagine making an impression of the *top* of your foot as well. Then when you put those top and bottom halves together, you create a *mold*. And when I pour this stuff . . ." he squished the phony finger, ". . . called latex into the empty space in the mold, it dries in the shape of whatever you want. See? Simple."

My mind was racing with the possibilities. "You mean, you could make, let's just say . . ." I held up my right hand, ". . . a copy of my hand?"

Garry smiled. "How long can you sit still?"

To help the latex dry, Garry keeps his workroom warm. So he flipped on a bunch of space heaters until it got to be about a hundred degrees in there. But, honestly? I hardly noticed the heat once Garry started working.

He had me cover my hand with oil so I wouldn't get stuck, and then he pressed my hand into a pan he had filled with a fluffy goo that looked like marshmallow cream. It felt kind of gross at first, but Garry made me promise not to move my hand while the goo was hardening, so I didn't.

And even though we later had to repeat the whole process with the *back* of my hand, I didn't get bored because Garry kept telling me awesome stories about the movies that he had built *effects* for back in North Carolina.

He talked about making a skull with a cleaver in it for *My Principal Is a Maniac!*, which I had actually seen on the Sci Fi Channel.

"You made the skull with the cleaver?" I gasped.

"That was mine," he blushed.

He described the swamp monster he created for *Honey, I Ate The Kids!* And there were about a dozen more that I'm forgetting now.

"And then, the *last* movie I did—the *very* last," he sighed, "was called *The Coming Of The Brain Biters*. Now, on the other films, I was one of a bunch of guys on the crew, but this one . . . this was entirely my baby. And this was a good story! It was about this evil alien bacteria that falls to earth. When people get it on their clothes, it eats into their skin and travels up to their brains and comes blasting out their eye sockets."

"Whoa!" My head was reeling. "I would *totally* see that movie."

"Right?" Garry was excited. "So I made all the alien bacteria and the brains and even the eyeballs." He picked up a perfectly painted eyeball from the counter and held it up proudly. "This was one."

I was stunned. "That's so good it's scary."

Garry smiled. "Thanks. Yeah. I did all the effects for every scene in the entire movie."

"You must've felt great," I said.

"Wait," Garry warned, holding up a hand. "Opening night. We stood in the back of a packed theater, ready to watch the audience jump out of their seats. And my first big moment came . . . the first big scare that was going to get the first big scream, and . . . and . . ."

He stopped.

"And?" I prompted.

Garry shook his head. "They laughed."

"You're kidding."

"No. They *laughed*. Just a few people at first. But that's all it took. Soon the whole audience was hooting and whistling and throwing popcorn at the screen. It was all over." He turned his face away.

"So what happened?"

He shrugged. "I left the theater. I went home. Packed my stuff. And I moved here."

"Maybe it wasn't your fault," I said.

"No," he sighed. "I had been working toward that moment since I was twelve. And nobody—not one person in that audience—freaked out. I just wanted to . . . to scare them. And I couldn't."

After a silence, he looked up at me. And he held up the eyeball.

"You want it?"

"Seriously?!"

"I don't need it anymore."

I took it, and all I could say was, "Whoa."

"Fortunately," Garry continued, "I have a college degree in business, so I fell back on that. I make a lot more money now, believe me. It was the best thing I could have done. Getting out of the effects business."

He got quiet for a second, and then he shook himself and said, "Speaking of 'getting out,' let's get you out of that mold." He pried my hand out of the hardening cast, and he took that mold and the one we'd made earlier over to a table where he set them in front of a space heater to finish their drying.

But the whole time Garry was busy with that, I was staring at the latex eyeball, hypnotized.

And I completely forgot about Garry making my "third hand."

I forgot about getting a theme for my party.

I forgot about making friends.

Because—and I know it sounds stupid—but at that moment I thought that eyeball was probably the most perfect present I had ever, ever received.

That night in bed I set the eyeball on my pillow, and I stared at it.

It reminded me of *Monsters & Maniacs*, Issue 114—"I Only Have Eyes for You—*FIVE HUNDRED OF THEM!!*"

And, as I lay there, I thought, *Wow. This eye will never blink. It will never sleep. It will always be watching me.*

And I fell asleep smiling.

16

I didn't really knock out Cougar. I know that's what people said, but the truth is that I never laid a hand on him.

I was alone at my cafeteria table the next day, playing games with my eyeball. Bouncing it. Winking it. Then I closed one eye and squeezed the fake one in under my eyebrow, like it was one of those single round eyeglasses that old men squint through in fancy English movies. I had just picked up a silverware knife to see my reflection in the blade when—WHAP!—I got smacked from behind, and I heard Cougar sneer, *"Made any cakes lately?"*

Cougar's slap snapped my head forward and sent my fake eyeball flying through the air toward an empty table, where it landed on a dirty plate in a little puddle of ketchup.

Cougar jerked his head toward the plate and ordered Scottie, "Hey. See what that is."

Scottie plucked the eye off the plate, and when he saw what he was holding, he freaked out! He quickly tossed the eyeball to Cougar, who looked down at this *thing* in his hand.

And it looked back at him.

It was still covered with ketchup, which I guess Cougar thought was real blood. He must have gotten scared that he had smacked my eyeball out of its socket, because that's when he gagged.

And his eyes rolled up into his head.

And he fainted.

No lie. Cougar went down like a sack of potatoes, taking a few empty lunch trays and a chair or two with him. The clattering made everyone stop what they were doing and turn.

And to them, it seemed like I had knocked Cougar out. The looks of admiration on the faces of my schoolmates were not looks that I was used to seeing, so I didn't hold up my hands and shout: "I didn't touch him!"

I figured I'd let them think what they wanted to.

Scottie and Mrs. Colby, the gym teacher, and I carried Cougar into the exam room of the School Nurse's office. The Nurse wasn't there, but a little paper clock on her door said, "BACK IN 5 MINUTES."

Mrs. Colby had to get back to gym class, so I volunteered to sit in the outside waiting room until the Nurse returned. Mrs. Colby said that that was very generous of me, and, after she sent Scottie back to class, she left, too.

It actually wasn't totally generous of me to wait with Cougar. See, when Cougar fainted, he squeezed my fake eyeball into his hand, and I knew that if I wanted it back, I had to be there when he opened his eyes.

The door to the exam room swung open, and I stood up to greet the Nurse. Instead, I was shocked to see Jennifer pop her head out and say, "He's coming around." She had a little white nurse's cap balancing on top of her red curls, and she was wearing a little white coat.

"*Jennifer?* What're you doing here?"

"Oh. I'm the Nurse's Aide."

"What does that mean?"

"Well, every day at fifth period, Nurse Dulaney goes behind the gym to have a cigarette, so I come in to watch the office. Mostly I just refill the Band-Aids," she admitted, but then she leaned close and confided, "but I'm trying to get her to let me draw blood."

There was a frightening thought.

Jennifer ushered me in to see Cougar. He was blinking and groggy, and what was really strange was that his forehead was covered with about twenty Band-Aids, stuck on in a crisscross pattern.

Jennifer jabbed Cougar's shoulder and barked:

"Get up, Leland. We need the bed."

"Don't call me 'Leland'!" Cougar snarled, and he swatted at her hand. Jennifer ignored him as she bustled in and out of the room, trying to look like she knew something about medicine.

When Cougar saw me his eyes got narrow. "You . . . !" was all he said. He wagged a finger at me, as if to say, *"I'm going to make you sorry."*

But then he realized that he had something in his hand; he opened his fingers and found . . . my eyeball. Smeared with ketchup.

"Uh . . . can I have that back?" I held out my hand. "Please?"

Cougar sat up on the exam table and squeezed the eyeball a few times to convince himself, I guess, that there was nothing to be afraid of. I could tell that he was fascinated, as fascinated as I had been when Garry first gave it to me.

"A bloody eyeball, hunh?" He looked up with a crooked smile. "You are so twisted, you know that?" And he started to laugh. I was so surprised to see him laughing without even hitting me first that I didn't know how to respond.

He held out the eyeball. "That is one scary idea, man," he said as he dropped it into my palm. And when I heard the word *idea*, I froze.

Wasn't it just yesterday that I was looking for someone with ideas? And now, without meaning to, had I actually come up with one?

A *scary* idea?

Scary idea, scary idea, scary idea tumbled around in my head like a marble in a clothes dryer. And by the time the eyeball landed in my hand . . .

. . . *I had my theme!*

Right then and there, I decided to throw a *Monsters & Maniacs* House of Horrors Happy-Birthday-to-you-Charley-Maplewood Party!!

It was brilliant!

It was inspired!

It was . . . !

"What the *heck?!*" Cougar stopped laughing because that's when he caught sight of himself in a wall mirror and was freaked out to find that he had, like, an entire box of Band-Aids stuck across his forehead.

Jennifer re-entered in time to hear his question.

"Those are for the bump on your head," she said in the crisp, professional way that she was practicing to be a nurse.

"There's no bump on my head, you . . . *cow!*"

Jennifer simply sniffed, "Oh. My bad." She reached up

and, with a lightning-fast flick of her wrist, Jennifer ripped the entire wad of Band-Aids off in one clean move.

Unfortunately, when they came off, so did Cougar's eyebrows.

People would later tell the story and snicker about how, at that moment, Cougar's scream had ripped through the halls and classrooms of the entire school, stopping everybody in their tracks.

But I didn't even flinch; I figured his eyebrows would grow back.

And besides, I had my theme.

MY THEME, MY CAKE
AND OTHER MISTAKES

17

I had to celebrate finding a theme, and I knew that if there was anybody in the whole world who would understand why I was so happy that afternoon, it would be Garry.

"You want me to *what?*" he asked when I got to his house.

"I want you to make a copy of my face. *Smiling.* So I can always remember this moment."

Garry was not accustomed to having people get so enthusiastic about being covered with slimy goo and sitting still for long periods of time, so he was actually kind of happy for the practice.

"Let's do it!" he said.

Garry clipped a towel around my neck and had me smear oil on the parts of my face where the marshmallow-creamy-stuff would be slopped on. He gave me two straws and explained that they'd have to go into my nose.

"You're not serious," I laughed.

"Fine. You don't have to. But when I spread on this goo, it'll fill your mouth and clog your nostrils and you'll suffocate. No big deal," he shrugged.

Ha ha. Very funny.

So I stuck the straws up my nose; I looked like a walrus with his tusks in the wrong place.

As Garry worked, I kept talking, and as I talked, I got more and more excited about my *Monsters & Maniacs* birthday party.

"I could have, like, skeletons at the door and skulls on the cake, y'know? And I'll get scary black napkins . . ."

"How," Garry wondered, "do you make black napkins *scary*?"

"Aha. Good point. But how's this? The punch could be red, like blood! Or green, like slime!"

See what I mean? The ideas were just pouring out of me.

"And, if you'd like," Garry offered, "I could lend you my DVD of *My Principal Is a Maniac!* to show at the party."

I sat up. "Get out!"

"Sit back!" Garry ordered, and pushed me down in the chair. "Are you gonna sit still?"

"I will. I promise. And you know why?" I said, settling down. "Because I've got a theme. Whoo-hoo!"

And then Garry covered my smiling face with goo.

I don't know how long I sat there—unable to see or speak— but from the way the goo warmed and tightened around my face, I could tell that Garry would have a really good mold to cast a mask from. I could hear him puttering around in his workshop, and when he'd ask, "You okay?" I would hold up my fingers in an "okay" circle.

I must have drifted off into a little nap, but I sure snapped wide awake the instant somebody started pounding at Garry's front door.

"Who in the world . . . ?" I heard Garry say. Then the pounding came again.

* * *

I guess when Garry opened his front door and found Mom standing there, he wasn't exactly looking spiffy. His hair was all in his eyes and his glasses were crooked. He had on his rubber apron and rubber gloves, and those were covered with the white goo that was hardening on my face at that very moment.

I could hear the whole conversation.

"I saw Boing Boing tied up on your porch. Is Charley here?"

"Huh? Oh, Charley. Yeah. He's . . . uh . . . he's sorta . . ."

"IS HE HERE?"

"He is. Yes."

"Charley?" Mom called into the house.

"But he's not . . . he can't . . ."

"Can you make a complete sentence?" When Mom asks something like that, you can tell she's about to lose it.

"He . . . can't come to the door right now."

"He what? Why not?"

"He's . . . well . . . it's about his head, see . . . ?"

"What about his head?"

"Not his head, actually. His face . . . it's covered up right now. But don't worry," Garry rushed to add, *"cuz he's got straws up his nose."*

"He's got WHATS up his nose?" And that's when I heard Mom push her way into the house. *"Charley? Charley, where are you?"* Her voice was getting closer. *"Where is he?"*

"In the garage," Garry was saying. *"But when you see him, don't get upset . . ."*

"Don't get upset? Why would I . . . OMIGOD!"

I figure that's when Mom saw me. I waved one hand in a friendly "hello," hoping to show her that I was okay, but it probably looked to her like Garry had buried me—with straws up my nose—under a mountain of mashed potatoes.

"What have you done to my son? Get him out of there!" I heard Mom shriek.

Garry pleaded, *"He just needs another minute . . . !"*

"NOW! Get him out now!"

And suddenly there were hands all over my face. *"Oh, please don't! NO!"* Garry shouted. I guess Mom was scratching and clawing at the hardened cast, as Garry was trying to save his work by peeling it up off my face from the edges.

I couldn't tell either one of them, "Stop! That hurts!" because my mouth was sealed shut; but, between their yelling and pushing and pulling and tearing, the mold finally released with a big sucking sound, and I saw daylight.

But "Ow ow ow ow ow ow ow!" was all I could manage to say.

"He wasn't *hurting me!*" I tried to explain as Mom dragged me and Boing Boing on his leash back to our house.

"Do you know how you scared me?" she wailed.

"But that's an *effect!* That's what Garry does! I told you—he's an *artist.*"

"I don't care if he's the President of the United States! I don't want you going over there. Never, ever again!"

"What? *Why?!*"

"Because!" Mom huffed. "That stuff is dangerous, and that man . . . that man is . . ."

"He's what?" I challenged her. "He might be my *friend*. And you said, 'You should make some friends.' "

"Well, then I *object* to your friend," Mom said.

"Oh, yeah? What about Vince? I object to *your* friend!" I responded.

Mom whipped around like I had poked her with a straight pin.

"Do you want a birthday party?!" she hissed at me, her face bright red. *"Do you?"*

I stopped breathing for a second, and my stomach flip-flopped. "You haven't sent out invitations yet!" Mom continued. "It would be so easy to just call the whole thing off. Just like *that!*" She snapped her fingers in front of my eyes.

And I swear I almost passed out.

18

I didn't feel like cooking that evening, so I boiled some hot dogs. Mom and I ate in silence.

As I chewed, I realized that she was right: it would be so easy to cancel a party that nobody's ever heard of. So what could I possibly do to prevent that?

And then an idea popped into my head that excited me so much I almost choked on my last bite of hot dog. In one blinding flash, I realized what I had to do to prevent Mom from cancelling my party.

I had to invite people.

In my bedroom after dinner I prepared to write my invitations. I would have liked to use black paper to announce my House of Horrors Birthday theme, but I didn't have any. And even if I did, none of my pens or pencils would have shown up on it.

So, instead, I cut up sheets of yellow and purple construction paper that I had left over from an Easter project our class did last year. I had eight squares of paper before I accidentally ripped one, but I told myself that was okay. Seven guests plus me made eight, and eight is enough. I didn't think Mom could object to that number.

With a red pen (which I hoped that people would understand was supposed to be blood) I drew lines on the invitations, and, with a thick black crayon, I started to write: "YOU ARE INVITED TO A HOUSE OF HOR—"

Then Mom tapped on my door.

I barely had time to slide the invitations under my school-books before she poked her head in and handed me the birthday card that Dad had sent.

"This fell out of your backpack."

I took the card, but I didn't say anything, hoping she'd get the hint and leave me alone.

"He thinks you're going to be eleven," she said with a little smile.

"Yeah," I nodded. "And he always gets the date wrong."

"That doesn't mean he doesn't love you," she was quick to point out.

I shrugged and looked away, and that worked, because after a moment, she left and shut the door.

I pulled out the invitations along with my Birthday Notebook, which I opened to the page where I had written:

3. FIND A THEME

Under that, I wrote with great pride: HOUSE OF HORRORS.

At the top of the page, however, under—

1. MAKE FRIENDS.

—there were still no names. I sighed.

"Doesn't matter," I told myself; my invitations were going to change all that. The next day seven of my classmates were going to receive an invitation to my birthday party.

Those seven would thank me with tears in their eyes.

Those seven would rush home to shout the news to their amazed families.

I just didn't know which seven they would be.

19

As I skateboarded to school the next morning with the invitations in my backpack, I knew I was going to have to be very careful about who I invited to my party. That way I could pick the perfect mix of personalities.

But things didn't work out that way.

And it was all Donna's fault.

I turned a corner in the hall and saw Donna at her locker, giggling and gossiping with Dana and Dina.

As always, she looked *amazing*.

I don't know what came over me; without even *thinking* about who the other six party-goers would be, I just stepped up and nervously held out an invitation to her.

"Oh. Hi, Charley," she said when she noticed me. Then she saw my piece of paper. "What's this?"

She took it, opened the folded purple page and, with Dina and Dana looking over her shoulder, she read what I had written.

" *'A House of Horrors Birthday Party'?*"

I nodded, tongue-tied.

Donna turned to Dina and Dana and chirped, "Whaddya think?"

Dana wrinkled her nose. "Mmm. I dunno."

Dina rolled her eyes and whined: "Sounds . . . *weird*."

So Donna made up their minds for them. "Sounds like fun to me!" she announced. And then you won't believe what she did. She plucked two more invitations from my pile and *handed them to her girlfriends!* She slammed her locker, said, "Thanks, Charley!" and they all walked away, laughing and tossing their hair.

It all happened so fast!

Even though I was just getting started, I had *only four in-vitations left.* And once Donna and Dina and Dana started blabbing, everybody, I was sure, would be after me. So my original plan—to pick my party-mates carefully—would have to be tossed right out the window.

Now I had to act quickly.

I caught up to Leo, limping along on his crutches. I held out a yellow page to him and babbled: "It's my birthday. I mean, it's gonna be. So, come, okay?"

Leo balanced on his crutches, took the paper, and shook my hand.

"Well, thanks, Charley. I'll do my best."

That went well, I thought.

I found Darryl Egbert in the upstairs boys' room. He unfolded the purple sheet and read my black crayon printing.

"*Horrors* has two R's," he said.

"Oh. Right," I muttered. "But what do you think?"

Darryl slipped the invitation into one of his books and pushed his glasses back on his nose. "I'll consult my parents, who will have to check their schedules," he said. "Saturdays are very busy days in our house."

And then he walked out. I'll admit I was expecting a more enthusiastic reaction.

But he didn't say "no."

Two.

I had two invitations left, and I intended to be very choosy about who was going to get them.

I could tell that word was spreading. As I stood at the door of the cafeteria at lunchtime, holding those two invitations and gazing out over the wide sea of possible party-goers, I felt that I, too, was being studied by hundreds of eyes, all eager to see my next move.

Then I heard: *"Hi, Charley,"* and my stomach dropped.

Jennifer Mobley was suddenly standing next to me, and her eyes were darting between me and the pieces of paper in my hand.

This was awkward.

But while I stood there, unable to think of what to say to Jennifer, the last two invitations were suddenly *snatched from my hand!*

"We checked our schedules, and we are free to party!" Cougar cackled. "I don't like onions on my hamburgers. And this guy," he said as he handed the last invitation to Scottie, "this guy's allergic to ice cream."

Cougar clapped me on the back. "But don't worry; we know how to have a good time!" Then they ran off, hooting.

And just like that, my party list was complete.

I was stunned.

Jennifer was as stunned as I was.

I gave a little shrug, as if to say, *"Oh, well."* She took a deep breath, smiled a tight little smile, and, without a word, she walked off. I knew her feelings were probably hurt, but what could I do? She saw what had happened!

So now, due to circumstances beyond my control, I was certain that I had just invited all the wrong people. My head was pounding as I kept seeing the same horrible picture in my mind:

Cougar and Scottie?!

In the same room with *Darryl?*

And *DONNA?!*

A House of Horrors Birthday Party?

I was scared already.

20

I almost caused about a dozen traffic accidents on my skateboard that afternoon because I was thinking so hard about the strange and, possibly, dangerous mix of people I would be bringing together for my party. When I turned onto our street, I was so distracted that I didn't notice Mom pulling up alongside me in her car. But I sure noticed when she rolled down her window and yelled, "Charley Maplewood!"

I tumbled off my skateboard, and we came to a stop in the street.

"What?"

"Did you hand out invitations at school today?" Mom didn't give me a chance to answer before she blasted ahead: "Because I got about a dozen calls at work. The parents of the kids you *did* invite are asking what their child should wear. And the parents of those you *didn't* invite are calling to say, 'You've ruined my kid's childhood!' "

Now, although I would never be happy about ruining somebody's childhood, I have to admit that I got a kick out of having created such a commotion.

"I am very upset," Mom was saying as she inched her car forward. "I'm not sure what I'm going to do with you. I'm actually inclined to . . ."

And I almost yelled, *"Please don't say you're going to cancel my party!"* But at that very moment, Mom leaned forward and squinted through her windshield.

"Now, what is *he* doing?" she asked.

I looked where she was looking, and I saw what she saw.

Garry was in our yard, down on his knees, and it looked like he had just finished replacing the mangled, dead bushes that Pincushion—I mean, *Stacy*—left behind when she ran over them on the night they broke up.

The new bushes were green and healthy, but that didn't matter to Mom. She pulled up in our driveway and got out of her car.

"This is our property, you know," she said sternly as she crossed to Garry.

He got to his feet and stuttered, "I . . . yeah. I feel bad about . . . y'know . . ." and he waved his hands at the hedge, ". . . so I've been meaning to . . . but . . ."

"That really isn't your concern," Mom cut him off.

He looked her in the eye and said very quietly, "But it was my fault."

That stopped Mom. After spending time with Garry, I already knew that he could make full sentences, but I think Mom was shocked that he could speak without tripping on his tongue.

"Oh? Oh. Okay. Well. Thank you," Mom stammered. She and Garry looked at each other in silence until finally Mom nodded and turned for home. But then she turned right back around.

"About that thing that happened in your garage yesterday . . ." she said to Garry while waving toward me, ". . . with Charley and the mask and my yelling and . . ."

"I know. I'm sorry. I should've asked," Garry said in a rush.

"Yes, you should have, but, still, I'm . . . ," and here Mom took a big breath, "I'm sorry I ruined your work. Charley tells me that's what you do."

"*Used to* do," he corrected her. Then he smiled. "But I might do it again!"

Which caused both Mom and me to say, "Oh?"

"Yeah. Yeah," Garry nodded, excited. "The Fresno . . . whatchamacallit . . . the Fresno Theater . . . place . . ."

"The Fresno Community Theater?" Mom suggested.

Garry pointed to her. "Them! Yeah. It's an interview. They want to see my work. For a play. It's not movies, but it's . . . y'know. What I do."

"That's nice. Congratulations," Mom said, and from the way she said it, I could tell she really meant it. "But I ruined some of your materials," she said, opening her purse, "and I'm sure that they're expensive, so I insist on paying for . . ."

"No!" Garry held up both hands. "Please. I had to order more anyway. Because of this interview I'm having. They asked me to make some scars."

Mom stopped digging through her purse and looked up. "Scars?"

"Mmm," Garry confirmed. "Scars. And a large stab wound. Who knows?" he shrugged. "Maybe I'll finally scare someone."

Mom nodded slowly as she backed away, "Oh. Okay. Well, good luck with that." And then she went into our house.

"I thought that went well," I said to Garry.

"Y'think?"

"Yeah. At least up to the part about the stab wound."

✳   ✳   ✳

As soon as I got into the house, Mom made me sit down at the kitchen table and write out a list of the people I had invited to my party.

"Seven," I said as I finished. "That's not a lot."

She wagged her head as she looked over the list. "I just wish you had talked to me before you did this." Then she looked up. "But the cat's out of the bag, so we'd better get cracking. Did we decide on a theme? Because the last I heard, it was cowboys, and . . ."

"No!" I stopped her. "Not cowboys."

"Then what?"

I hesitated. Something told me that I couldn't just blurt out about the House of Horrors.

"There are . . . several ideas on the table," I said carefully.

"Get rid of all but one," she said. "And then go see Vince."

Uh-oh.

"Can't I go to another cake store?"

"Do you know how much he's saving us by doing your cake?" Mom said sharply. But she could tell that I was upset, so she pulled out a chair and sat down with me.

"Look, Charley. I know how you feel about Vince. But he's just a lonely, divorced man, looking for a friend. Like I am. Offering to make your cake . . . that's just his way of reaching out. So. Will you go see him?"

Mom tilted her head in that way that says, *"Please?"* So I nodded.

"Thank you," Mom whispered. She stood, kissed me on the forehead, and started out of the kitchen.

I stopped her with, "See? Garry's not so creepy."

She took a breath and held it as she tried to decide what to say. "Honey. He made a nice gesture. But he's still a profoundly strange man." Then she left.

But I smiled. Because I could tell that she wasn't scared of Garry anymore.

Not like before.

"If I had money, I would go to some bakery where they didn't know me and order the cake I want," I was saying to Garry that evening. I had seen him out in his backyard, washing the tools that he uses to make his *effects,* so I went outside and climbed onto the roof of Boing Boing's doghouse.

I know, I know. Mom had said that she didn't want me going over to Garry's. But she didn't say I couldn't talk to him over the fence.

"But this guy . . . Vince?" Garry was saying as he hosed off his gear. "Maybe he's tired of cowboy cakes, too. Maybe he'll like your theme."

"But what if he *hates* my theme, and he calls Mom, and she says 'no'?"

"When were you planning to tell her?" Garry asked.

I hadn't even thought of that. "I don't know, I don't know!" I wailed as I shook my head in despair. "Why is life so hard?"

Garry snickered.

"No, really!" I insisted. "I'm afraid to tell Mom. I'm afraid to tell Vince. Maybe I should just forget the whole thing."

"Don't!" Garry said quickly. He looked me in the eye. "Do *not* let fear rule your life, Charley. I made that mistake."

"When you quit?" I asked.

"When I . . . *left*," he said softly, and then he looked away.

Even in the fading evening light, I could see that Garry was thinking about North Carolina again, so I jumped down off Boing Boing's roof and left Garry alone with his thoughts.

21

Once I finished my homework that evening, I got down on the floor of my room and, from under my bed, I pulled out the plastic storage bins containing my collection of *Monsters & Maniacs*. With Boing Boing sleeping in my lap, I carefully studied every cover of every issue I own, trying to find the perfect picture to show Vince so that he could have the baker and the frosting guy at The Paradise Pantry put it on my birthday cake.

I narrowed the choice down to two:

The cover of Issue 48 ("The Car of Tomorrow . . . It Seats Four AND *EATS MANY MORE!!!*") has always been one of my favorites. It's a picture of a family being chewed up and swallowed by a car's hood (because the car runs on human flesh instead of gasoline, see?). I swear you can practically hear the people screaming.

But I couldn't decide between that one and an old classic: Issue 12, one of the first *Monsters & Maniacs* I ever owned. Even though the story isn't one of the creepiest ("My Daddy *IS A MUMMY!*"), there's something about the way the bandages are rotting off the smiling corpse on the cover that still gives me chills.

Both pictures are so awesome that I couldn't make up my mind. So, the next morning at school, I put it to a vote.

*   *   *

"Which one would look better on top of a cake?" I asked Cougar and Scottie, holding up the comic books for their consideration. I had made them follow me to a deserted end of the schoolyard so that no one else would learn about the final choice.

But instead of taking this decision seriously, Scottie and Cougar looked at each other and cracked up.

"What?" I was irritated. "What's so funny?"

Scottie shook his head. "It's just so lame, man!"

"What is?"

"This whole House-of-Horrors thing, Doofus!" Cougar cackled. "I mean, you're *telling* people that you're gonna scare 'em, and then you're actually gonna *try* to scare 'em? Good luck!" he said as they started to walk away.

"Well, you don't have to come!" I shouted at their backs.

"Are you kidding?" Cougar didn't even bother turning around. "We wouldn't miss it for the world."

I caught the Mealiffe Avenue bus after school, because The Paradise Pantry is too far to skateboard to. As I sat on the bus, my knee kept bouncing up and down; I had decided to go with the flesh-eating car as my birthday cake choice, but now I was just really, really nervous about how Vince would react.

The bus dropped me off right in front of The Paradise Pantry, which, I have to admit, is a lot fancier than the Happy Giant Supermarket where I shop. They've got white and blue striped awnings out front, and the staff all wear white shirts and blue aprons and smile a lot.

When I walked in the front door, I asked a cash-register lady where I could find Mr. Champagne, and she pointed me back toward Frozen Foods. I took a deep breath, and I started to walk.

While I had been on the bus, I had planned how I would handle this moment. I was going to find Vince, walk right up to him and give him a really squeezy handshake. I thought that he might like that, especially because he taught me how to do it. I was running this scene over in my head, when I turned a corner and I saw Vince. And I froze. Right there in Frozen Foods.

Because he was with somebody. Not just *with* somebody. He was hugging her.

A lady with a shopping cart. A shopping cart with a little girl in the kid's seat. He was hugging the lady, and they were giggling, and she was pretty.

Then a man carrying a crate of tomatoes walked past, and he joked, "Hey, Vince! Is that your way of keeping the customers happy?"

Vince stopped hugging the lady, turned to the Tomato Man and laughed, "Eddy, c'mon! You've met my wife."

I heard it with my own two ears. *"You've. Met. My. Wife."*

If the floor could have opened at that moment and swallowed me, I wouldn't have minded.

I guess I gasped, because that's when Vince looked up and saw me standing there. Close enough to have seen and heard everything that had just happened. And the way his jaw dropped, I could tell that I had seen something I wasn't supposed to.

I think Vince started toward me, but I'm not sure. The next thing I can honestly remember was being outside, running down the sidewalk as fast as my legs could carry me.

I ran for blocks and blocks. Miles, probably. The whole time I was running, I was hoping I could run far enough that I'd never have to go back and tell Mom what I'd seen, or—worse yet—go back and pretend that I hadn't seen anything at all.

But my stomach started to ache, and my backpack, with my skateboard and comic books inside, was banging real hard on my spine, and, eventually, I slowed down. I wandered around until I stopped shaking inside.

Then I took a deep breath, and I headed home.

22

When I walked into the kitchen, Mom was standing at the sink, staring out into the backyard. She didn't turn around to greet me.

Then I noticed that Lorena was sitting in silence at the kitchen table in her Chick-A-Dee uniform, and she was a mess. She had smears of mashed potatoes and gravy on her blouse; her mascara was running down her cheeks; and she had gobs and gobs of coleslaw in her hair.

I waited for one of them to speak, but nobody did. Finally I turned to Lorena.

"What happened to you?"

She sneered. "Brad grabbed my butt again. So I stabbed him in the hand with a fork, like you said."

"Seriously?" I was actually sort of pleased that *Monsters & Maniacs* had provided Lorena with a real-life solution.

"Then I threw a Cluck Bucket at him. So he threw a super-size soda at me. And a carton of coleslaw. Before you know it . . ." She waved her hand at all the food she was wearing. "And then he fired me."

"Wow," was all I could manage.

"Men are such scum," Lorena groaned as she put her head down on the table.

That's when Mom spoke for the first time: "Tell me about it."

At that moment I realized that she knew. About Vince.

She turned to me. "Vince called. After you left." She shook her head sadly. "I thought he was single."

And that was that. We didn't talk any more about Vince. Or Lorena getting fired.

Instead, Mom did what she usually does when she's upset. She went upstairs and changed into her doing-chores-around-the-house clothes. Then she dragged the folding stepladder out to the back porch, where a section of roof gutter had been needing repairs for months.

And, as I chopped and stirred in the kitchen, I could hear the whine of Mom's electric screwdriver long after it got dark.

There's a soup I make with canned corn that Mom calls "Charley's Comfort Chowder," so I made a pot of that, even though nobody felt like sitting down to dinner that evening. When it was ready, I took a cup of it out to Mom.

She was way up on the stepladder. I had to wait for the screwdriver noise to stop before I said, "I made Comfort Chowder. You hungry?"

She shook her head "no." But she didn't go back to working; instead, she sighed and said, "I feel so . . . *stupid*, Charley."

I nodded. "Mmmm. I feel that way a lot."

She smiled a teensy smile.

I had planned to wait until morning to bring something up, but the moment seemed right, so I asked: "Can I still have my birthday party?"

Mom looked surprised. "Why wouldn't you?"

"Because," I shrugged. "Because we don't have a free cake anymore."

"Then you'll just have to make one. I bet your friends will be impressed."

I appreciated her confidence in my cooking skills, but I could never create the *Monsters & Maniacs* cake of my dreams.

I was snapped out of my pity-party when Mom gave a little gasp and smacked her forehead. "Oh, honey! I completely forgot. I've got something for you. Something *wonderful!*"

Mom hurried into the house, and I followed. She was explaining, "I started getting into the spirit today. The birthday spirit . . ." as we went up to her bedroom, ". . . so! I went shopping during my lunch break. And what do you think I found?"

By now, we were standing at the foot of Mom's bed, and she was holding up a shopping bag that she had pulled from inside her closet door.

"This was going to be a surprise, but this is as good a time as any for cheering ourselves up, isn't it?"

I nodded eagerly.

Mom emptied the shopping bag onto her bedspread. And when I saw what tumbled out, I just about collapsed.

I was staring down at eight miniature cowboy hats with elastic chinstraps; a plastic bag full of plastic cowboys and plastic horses; napkins with pictures of cows on them; paper plates with lassoes printed around the edges; and a paper tablecloth covered with drawings of bucking broncos and *cacti*.

"I just went to browse, and I couldn't help myself! I got such a kick out of buying it all," Mom was chattering away as I stared in shock. "Come to think of it, it's the one nice thing that happened all day."

She turned to me with a big smile and said, "What do you think?"

I didn't answer right away, because I knew I had a choice: I could either break down and tell Mom about the House of Horrors birthday that I had promised everybody, and, by doing so, I would probably crush her spirits.

Or, I could say what I said.

"Oh, cool. Cowboys."

23

"Is it true? *Is it true?!*" Jennifer Mobley was panting with excitement as she raced down the hallway toward me, hair flying, braces sparkling.

"Is what true?"

"You're throwing a *House of Horrors Birthday Party?!* I know I'm not invited or anything, but I hear people talking, and I just gotta ask you . . ."—she lowered her voice—". . . how're you going to do it, Charley? How're you going to scare people? Can you give me a hint? Just a little one?"

I winced at her questions, and she quickly stepped back. "Oh, okay! I totally understand. You don't have to tell me now and ruin the surprise. But maybe you can take pictures and make notes, and tell me afterwards? Huh? Please? Promise?"

"I don't know," I mumbled as I busied myself with schoolbooks. "I'm thinking now that maybe it's not such a good theme. Maybe I should change it."

Jennifer's mouth flew open with shock. "What? You can't change it! Your theme is . . . is *genius!*"

I almost said "Really? You think so?" but just then, from behind us, Cougar spoke: *"He can't change what?"*

We turned to find that Cougar and Scottie had been eavesdropping.

"He's gonna change his birthday theme!" Jennifer practically exploded to Cougar, momentarily forgetting that she never speaks to him.

Cougar clapped me on the shoulder. "Oh, man. We gotta talk."

"Excuse me?" Jennifer said to Cougar, pointing between herself and me. "*We're* already talking here."

"Oh, I believe you are through," Cougar sneered.

"I don't believe we are," Jennifer sneered back.

"Hmm. That's odd," said Cougar pensively. He stuck a finger in his nose, pulled it out and examined his fingernail. "Cuz this *booger* says that you *are* through."

And when he thrust his finger at Jennifer's face, she threw up her hands, shrieked, *"Ew, Leland!"* and ran off down the hall.

Cougar swiped his finger on his jeans and turned to me. "So, what's goin' on?"

"I'm . . . I'm having second thoughts," I said weakly. "About my party theme."

"What kind of second thoughts?" Cougar's eyes narrowed with suspicion. "Cuz I'm telling you right now—you'd better not have a clown."

"Clowns give him nightmares," Scottie sniggered to me.

"That was only one time!" snapped Cougar. He turned back to me. "And don't even think about cowboys."

"Eww! Cowboys . . . blecch!" Scottie stuck out his tongue in disgust.

So I sure wasn't going to tell them what Mom had already bought.

"Look, man," Cougar suddenly sounded threatening. "You announced a House of Horrors party. You better at least *try* to scare people."

"Yeah," Scottie nodded. "Even if you can't."

"But it's not easy!" I blurted out. "Scaring people."

Cougar shook his head. "Oh, I dunno. That bloody-eyeball-thing of yours had me going pretty good."

"Yeah!" Scottie snorted, punching Cougar's arm. "You went down like a ton of bricks!"

"Shut up!" Cougar barked and punched him back twice as hard.

But while they sparred, I stood there with my jaw dropping, because what Cougar said had just sent a bolt of inspiration crashing into my brain!

You think a single eyeball is scary? I thought. *What about seeing a severed foot floating in a punch bowl? Or finding a bloody ear in your slice of birthday cake? Or . . .* My explosion of ideas was interrupted when Cougar turned back to me.

"Look, Charlie, we're coming to your birthday party like *we* promised. And if you know what's good for you, you'll throw the party . . ." he jabbed his booger finger in my face, ". . . that *you* promised."

24

I truly believed that Cougar's comment held the key to my salvation: body parts can be very scary, especially when not attached to a body.

And I knew where to get some!

My heart was pounding like a jackhammer as I raced home that afternoon, because I was painfully aware that the plan I was formulating—although *brilliant*—wasn't perfect.

For one thing, I had no idea how I was going to break the news to Mom that my party theme would no longer be "cowboys."

And since she had forbidden me to ever go over to Garry's again, how was I going to explain to her where I got a shopping bag full of latex body parts?

Still, my idea was burning a hole in my skull, and I had to act on it immediately. I was only planning to borrow a few *effects* from Garry and worry about the rest later.

That's all I had in mind.

Honest.

I never planned to burn down our garage.

Of all the afternoons to leave the house, Garry had picked the worst possible one. I pounded on his front door for about five minutes before I accepted the fact that he wasn't at home. I was so deep in thought about what to do next that I didn't hear the delivery van pull up at Garry's curb.

When I turned around and found the Delivery Man standing right behind me, I yelped like a dog when a door closes on his tail.

"Sorry. Didn't mean to scare you," said the Delivery Man.

"You didn't scare me," I lied.

He read the label of a box he was carrying: "Got a delivery here from Stage Effects Latex for Garry Quarky. You know him?"

I didn't answer right away, because I was staring at the box. And—call me crazy—but, from the size of it, I was willing to bet that there was enough latex in there to make a whole lot of scary body parts.

And, because I had watched Garry, I knew *exactly how to do just that!*

"Kid?"

"Huh?" I blinked, trying to remember what the question was.

"Do you know this Garry Quarky guy?" he asked, nodding at Garry's house.

"Garry? Oh, sure. We're buddies." I pointed to my house. "I live right there."

"You wanna sign for the package, then?" the Delivery Man asked. And he held the box out to me.

Can you imagine my state of mind? *I was being offered the opportunity of a lifetime.* Mom would be home by the end of the afternoon. Garry may not be. I might never have this chance again!

And though a little voice in my head was chattering, *"That latex is not yours!"* it was being drowned out by an even louder voice that was chanting: *"Birthday! Birthday! Birthday!"*

"Sure, I'll sign!" I said suddenly.

And, with a flick of a pen, my fate was sealed.

I waited until the delivery van had turned the corner at the end of our street before I ran around into Garry's backyard. Sure enough, Garry had left a lot of his tools out to dry, so I borrowed the ones that I guessed I would need—including the molds for making a finger, an ear and a nose.

Then I raced home and opened Garry's box in our garage. I realized that I was taking something that wasn't mine, but, because I was sure that Garry would understand my crisis, it didn't feel like stealing.

Besides, wasn't Garry the one who told me not to let fear rule my life?

So I was not afraid.

Sure enough, the delivery box contained four tall, plastic jars of white, gooey latex. If I could just work fast enough, I thought, I could be finished by the time Mom got home from work. Pouring the latex into the molds was going to be a snap; it was waiting for it to dry that was going to take time.

But then I remembered how Garry had flicked on portable floor heaters to make his workshop really warm and speed up the drying process. Just by luck, we have a space heater that Mom stores under the stairs when it's not winter. I ran and grabbed it, snatched up a couple of paper towels—in case I spilled anything—and rushed back into the garage.

I was ready to start molding.

* * *

"Why is it so hot in here?" Lorena whined, leaning into the garage.

"Close the door!"

I was kneeling on the floor in front of the portable heater, concentrating on keeping my very first molded finger warm. I probably looked like a mother hen fussing over an egg.

"What're you doing?" Lorena asked.

"What do you want?" I shot back. Ever since she got fired from the Chick-A-Dee, Lorena had been hanging around the house a lot more than she used to.

"Well, when you work at the Chick-A-Dee, you're not allowed to date fellow employees, y'know?" she started to explain.

"So?"

"So. Ever since Brad fired me, he's been begging me to go out with him. Like, today he called my cell phone about a hundred times."

I turned and used one of her own lines on her: "You speak to me as if I care."

"Ha ha, very funny," Lorena scoffed. "Anyway, I hate Brad. So if he shows up, don't answer the door."

I could feel the temperature in the room dropping with every passing second.

"Get out!" I finally shouted.

"Whatever you're doing, Mom's gonna kill you," Lorena said as she slammed the door and stomped away.

It was a little hard getting the first finger to plop out of the mold. I think it was sticky because I had rushed the process, but

I was learning from my mistakes and still confident that I could crank out a bunch more body parts before Mom got home.

Then, from inside the house, I heard the ding-dong-ding-dong-ding-dong of our doorbell being pushed over and over again.

"*Loreeeeeeena!*" Brad was wailing on our porch.

"*Go home, Brad!*" Lorena screamed from somewhere upstairs.

"Oh, *please* go home, Brad," I groaned under my breath.

Brad resumed ringing and pounding, and I heard Lorena's footsteps racing down the stairs to the front door.

"*Get away from my door, Brad! I hate you!*"

"*Can we talk? I just want to talk to you.*"

"*No. GO AWAY!*"

"*Please?*" Brad begged. Then, in a little boy voice, he added, "*Pweeeeez? Pwetty pwease?*"

Lorena is a sucker for guys who do little boy voices.

"Don't open the door, don't open the door, don't open the door," I murmured, hoping to influence Lorena's behavior with mind-power. (Like in *Monsters & Maniacs* Issue 93: "The Man With Two Brains . . . *HIS AND YOURS!!!*")

But it didn't work. In the silence that followed I figured out that Lorena was melting like a sno-cone in July, because the next sound I heard was the front door opening.

"*What do you want, Brad?*" huffed Lorena.

"*Will you come out and pway wid me?*" Brad whined.

Lorena sighed, "*Awwwww, Brad,*" and then I heard nothing for about a minute.

Until, suddenly, Lorena *screamed* like her fingernails were being pulled out with pliers!

Now, Lorena and I may have a lot of differences, but she's still my sister. That's why I jumped up from my post in front of the heater, yelled, "LORENA!" and knocked over everything in my path on my way out. I threw open the garage door, raced to the front hall, and, with Boing Boing yelping right behind me, I ran out onto the front lawn, where Lorena and Brad were having a terrible fight.

At least that's what it looked like to me.

He had her by the hair and, as she struggled to get free of his vicious grip, they were thrashing all over the lawn while Lorena kept yelling, "Ow! Brad! Stop! Ow!"

I flew at Brad, pounding him, screaming, "Leave my sister alone!" At the same time, Boing Boing was leaping and snapping at him from the other side. There was a lot of noise, and everybody was shouting, "Ouch!" and "Stop!" and "Don't!" until Lorena snorted at me, "Give it a rest, you dork!"

"But he's hurting you!" I pointed out. In fact, Brad's fist was *still* buried in my sister's hair.

"No, he's not," she scoffed. "I'm stuck."

She twisted her head around to show me that her hair was tangled in the buckle of Brad's wristwatch; I guess he had tried to run his fingers through her hair, and he'd gotten stuck.

"Oh," was all I could manage to say.

I thought I should at least get credit for coming to Lorena's rescue, even if she didn't need rescuing; but Lorena and Brad were too busy giggling and untangling her hair from his wristwatch buckle to give me a second thought.

So I stood there on our front lawn, feeling stupid and useless; Boing Boing stared up at me with a look that said, *"That was fun. What's next?"*

And that's when our neighbor Mrs. Cleveland came tearing out of her house, waving her golf-club-walking-stick over her head and wailing, "Fire! Fire! Save yourselves!" And she was pointing *to our garage.*

Brad, Lorena, Boing Boing and I all turned and saw the smoke at the same time.

And my very, very short life flashed before my eyes.

It was a little fire, I promise. There were no big yellow and red flames licking at the walls. But, still, it was a fire.

By the time the fire trucks came squealing up our little street with their sirens shrieking, neighbors from blocks around were standing and staring at the black smoke billowing out of our garage.

Mom was coming home from work when a policeman stopped her at the end of our street. She jumped from her car and sprinted down the block, pushing through the crowd and panting, "That's my house! My children are in there!"

When she saw that Lorena and I were okay, she looked like she was going to cry or faint, but before she did either one, Lorena pointed to me and said, "It's his fault."

And it was. Sort of.

The firemen had told us that when I jumped up and ran out of the garage, I had knocked a paper towel in front of the portable heater that was warming my finger mold; the heater lit the paper towel on fire, and it spread from there.

But I wouldn't have jumped up if Lorena hadn't screamed.

And Lorena wouldn't have screamed if Brad had stayed away.

So, see? There was plenty of blame to go around.

A little while later, Garry came shoving through the crowd, totally out of breath from running down the street.

"Is everybody okay?" he asked us all, but he looked at Mom as he spoke.

"It seems you've given my son some very dangerous ideas," Mom said before she turned her back and walked away, leaving me to face Garry.

"What did she mean by that?" he asked.

I hung my head.

"Well, I . . . uh . . ." I started softly. "I was trying to make some body parts. With your latex. And I turned on the heater so they'd . . ."

"Wait a minute, wait a minute!" Garry waved his hands. "*My* latex?"

I nodded.

Garry glanced back at his house, then at me. "How'd you get your hands on *my* latex?"

"The Delivery Man . . . he let me sign for your box."

Garry blinked once and stared at me in silence. It was horrible.

"But don't you want to know why I was making body parts?"

"No," he said gravely. "I don't."

We stood like that for a few more terrible moments before he crossed to Mom and started to say, "I had no idea what Charley was up to. If there is anything that I can . . ."

But Mom flipped up her hand in a way that said, *"Stop!"* So he did.

Garry glanced over at me and shook his head. Then he crossed his lawn, went into his house, and shut his door. And when he did, my eyes started to burn.

And it wasn't from the smoke.

25

After the firemen drove away and our neighbors all returned to their homes, Brad kissed Lorena good-bye and went to work at the Chick-A-Dee.

Boy, did I feel dumb. Even a blind man could see that she didn't *really* hate him.

The garage was still standing. A few boxes of Christmas decorations had burned, and some of our garden tools were too melted to ever use again. But it could have been a lot, lot worse.

That didn't matter to Mom.

Neither did the fact that I said, "Sorry," about five hundred times in the next few hours.

That evening, as we were throwing out all the charred and water-soaked remains of the fire, Mom looked around at the damage, shook her head and muttered, "We don't have the money for this."

Then she took a deep breath to make herself feel brave, and I could tell she had already made a plan.

"I talked to Mr. Fittipaldi, and he's gonna let me add some Saturdays to my schedule. Pick up a little extra cash."

She was already sounding better.

"But, Charley," Mom turned to me, "if I work Saturdays, I can't be here for your birthday party."

I stopped breathing.

"He doesn't deserve one after what he did," snarled Lorena.

"Hey!" Mom snapped at her. "Your brother ran out to help you."

Lorena bit her lip.

"So, Charley," Mom continued, "I'm going to have to call everyone's parents and tell them that the party is off."

"No!" I cried out.

" '*No*'?" Mom asked sharply.

She and Lorena stared at me until I dropped my head and mumbled, "I . . . I should tell them myself."

"See that you do," Mom said. "See that you do."

26

When I got to school the next morning, Donna and Dina and Dana smiled at me from their lockers; I couldn't bring myself to un-invite them first. Then Leo gave me a thumbs-up. And Darryl waved. How could I ruin their day with my bad news?

It was only when I saw Cougar and Scottie bearing down on me in the hallway that I knew where I was going to start.

"Hi, guys," I gulped and waved. "Listen. About my party. . . ."

Cougar stopped and squinted at me. "What about your party?"

"It's just . . . there may . . . there might be a teensy problem."

Cougar grabbed my collar and slammed me up against a locker.

"Don't tell me you're getting a clown."

"No," I grunted. "No clowns."

"So what's the problem?" Scottie asked.

The locker knob was digging into my back, and Cougar's grip on my neck was cutting off my flow of oxygen, so I decided not to un-invite them just yet.

"Oh," I shrugged. "Nothing I can't handle."

Cougar released me and clapped me on the shoulder. "That's my man! Okay, check this out." He looked behind us to make sure we weren't being watched, and then he pulled a small aerosol can from his jacket pocket and held it up for me to see.

"Spray glue. Stole it from my dad."

From the way he proudly displayed it, I figured out that stealing a can of spray glue from one's dad was some kind of awesome accomplishment.

"Whoa." I looked between him and Scottie. "What's it for?"

Cougar snickered in his crazy way.

"Wait'll you hear this plan he's got," Scottie snorted. "It's the best."

Jennifer Mobley looked up when I entered the Nurse's Office. She was wearing her little white coat, and her little white nurse's cap was balancing on her explosion of hair.

"Hi, Charley!" she said brightly, but her smile faded when Cougar and Scottie stepped in behind me.

"The Nurse is out," said Jennifer sourly. "What're you guys doing here?"

I turned to Cougar. "Yeah. What *are* we doing here?"

"Well, you're here to be our lookout," he said as he grabbed my arm and pushed me halfway out the doorway.

"I'm your *what?*" I sputtered.

"Just tell me when somebody's coming," he ordered in a loud whisper.

"Why? What're you gonna do?" I demanded.

"Hey!" Cougar pointed a stern finger in my face. "You wanna be our friend, doncha?"

The question paralyzed me. Because he was right; after a lifetime of not really thinking about it, I now wanted to be somebody's friend. Even Cougar's.

He turned and snatched Jennifer's nurse's cap off her head.

"Leland, give that back!" she wailed, reaching for her cap.

"Scottie!" Cougar shouted, and Scottie jumped in front of Jennifer, waving his arms like he was guarding a basketball star with the ball.

"Get out of my way, Scottie!" Jennifer demanded. "I am *the Nurse's Aide!*"

As she struggled to get past Scottie, Cougar pulled out his can of spray glue and popped off the top. He was moving so fast that I couldn't have stopped him, even if I could have figured out what he was up to.

"What're you doing with that?!" Jennifer squealed.

Cougar pointed to the place on his face where his eyebrows used to be, before Jennifer ripped them off.

"It's payback time," he chortled, and then he coated the inside of Jennifer's nurse's cap with a sweeping, wet spray of glue.

"Stop that! Leland! Give me back my hat this instant!"

"Whatever you say," Cougar sneered as he finished spraying. Then he smooshed the hat down on Jennifer's hair. And he held it there.

Jennifer gasped.

I gasped.

Cougar and Scottie cackled.

For a long, horrified moment I stood there thinking: *I have to do something. But what?! WHAT?!*

So I blurted out the only thing that came rushing into my brain.

"I hear somebody coming!"

In a split second, Cougar and Scottie were out the door. I was frozen in place, though, watching Jennifer wincing and tugging at the cap that was now firmly bonded to her wild thatches of hair.

She looked up and caught my eye, but just as I opened my mouth to *swear* to her that I had no idea Cougar had planned such a terrible revenge, Scottie grabbed my elbow, hissed, "Let's go, Jerkface!" and yanked me down the hall.

27

I hid out in the upstairs boys' room for the rest of the day. From time to time, I splashed water on my face and stared in the mirror. *"What has happened to you?!"* I silently asked the monster I had become.

I waited until the school emptied and the halls had gone silent. By the time I left the building, only the janitors were left.

I set my skateboard down and was about to step on it when I realized: *no!* I didn't deserve to go zipping along, carefree and untroubled. Not after what I had done. So I picked up my skateboard and trudged toward home. At the far end of the block, I turned the corner, and what I saw nailed my feet to the sidewalk.

Across the street, Jennifer Mobley sat alone on a bus stop bench. I cringed when I noticed that her once poofy hair had been lopped off in more than a few patches.

Seeing her hunched over like that, intently studying her homework, I felt worse than I had felt since . . . well, since the night before when Garry shook his head and walked away from me. And I suddenly knew how Jennifer felt.

Because in that moment I knew what it was like to lose a friend.

See, I was so new to the whole friendship thing that I'd

never really known somebody—outside my family—who could hurt my feelings the way Garry had.

Or someone whose feelings I could hurt the way I'd hurt Jennifer.

I couldn't go home feeling so rotten.

When I sat down at the other end of her bus stop bench, Jennifer glanced out of the corner of one eye. Neither one of us breathed.

"Did you come to laugh some more?"

"There's nothing funny," I said quietly.

After a long silence, she pointed to her head.

"Nurse finally came back. She cut me out of my hat."

"Oh," I nodded. "You can't tell."

She looked up and studied my face. Her eyes were red, like she had recently been crying, but, from the way she finally nodded, I could tell that she believed me. Then she went back to studying.

Now I should say something nice, I thought. *But what?* Mom says that "I'm sorry" is always appreciated, but that's only two words; the horrible trick that I had been a part of would need a lot more words to make right, I felt.

What could we talk about? *Monsters & Maniacs?* The weather? Her job in the Nurse's Office? Not one of them seemed right for the moment.

But I had to say *something*.

Okay, you know how sometimes your mouth can say words that your brain wasn't even planning on? And when they fly out and you hear them out there in the world, you can't *believe* what you've just said?

That's what I did.

"Jennifer?"

She looked up.

"Yeah?"

"You wanna come to my birthday party?"

28

I know, I know! Dumb, Dumber, Dumbest! I was all three.

I *knew* my birthday party had been cancelled.

I *knew* I was supposed to be un-inviting my guests.

And I *knew* that, without Mom's help, I could never *ever throw a party on my own!!!*

But when, very quietly, Jennifer answered, "I would like that, Charley," you know what?

I knew I had to.

So my birthday party was back on again.

I felt pretty great about my wild decision almost all the way home, until I stopped in the middle of traffic when a terrifying realization hit me: *now I would need a cake.* And napkins. And noisemakers. And decorations. And all those things cost money!

But I had none.

Without a job, neither did Lorena. Garry wasn't speaking to me. And I sure couldn't ask Mom.

So how could I possibly get some cash in the two weeks until my birthday?

That night I fell asleep with that question burning my brain; I tossed and turned in distress until, about three A.M., I woke up with an idea that was so amazing—and so horrible at the same time—that I didn't know whether to jump up and down or to curl up and cry.

I would sell my *Monsters & Maniacs.*

I mean, comic books are *big business*, right? There's always some story in the news about a collector—of comic books or coins or baseball cards or something—who sells his entire "lifetime collection" and gets paid enough money to buy a big jet and a small island. So I knew I was sitting on a gold mine.

When I made up my mind, I felt like I'd been punched in the stomach, but I also knew that selling my comics was the only possible solution.

The next day after school, I loaded my plastic bins of *Monsters & Maniacs* into Mom's wheelbarrow and rolled them over to The Comic Soup, where I had bought them in the first place. And though I was sad, my head was spinning with visions of all the birthday goodies I would now be able to buy with the stacks of cash I would soon hold in my hot little hands.

Unfortunately, the staff at The Comic Soup didn't see things that way.

Gene the Bean—he's called that because he's tall and skinny, and because he dyes his long, stringy hair green—looked over my booty and called across the racks and racks of comics.

"Hey, Zandar, check it out: Charley's selling his stash."

Zandar is the other clerk at The Comic Soup; "Zandar" is not his real name, but he read it in a comic book when he was, like, eight, and he's been Zandar ever since.

"Ooh, what've we got here?" Zandar asked, scratching his big belly through his *Star Trek* T-shirt.

"It's all my *Monsters & Maniacs*," I said proudly. "A life-time collection."

Zandar and Gene the Bean burst out laughing.

"What?" I asked.

"Charley," chuckled Zandar. "You're what? Seven? Eight?"

"I'm nine," I said, defiant.

"Even so," explained Gene the Bean, "that's not much of a lifetime. What I mean to say is: your 'lifetime collection's' not much of a collection."

I was stunned. "So, wait! You don't want to buy them?"

They both shrugged.

"You come back after collecting for thirty or forty years," said Zandar, "and I promise we'll pay you a bundle."

I hung my head. "I can't wait that long."

"Why do you want to sell them anyway?" asked Gene the Bean. "*Monsters & Maniacs* is truly smokin'!"

"I need money," I said. "For my birthday party. Next Saturday's my Big One-Oh."

"Whoa," they both sighed. Then they exchanged a *"what a shame!"* look and shook their heads.

Before they could pity me any more, I picked up the wheelbarrow handles and was starting out of the store when Zandar suddenly called out, "Hey, wait a second, Charley!" He turned to Gene the Bean, snapping his fingers. "That phone call you got . . . that collector in Chicago? What was he looking for?"

"Oh! Right you are!" exclaimed Gene the Bean. He rushed behind the counter and grabbed a note that had been taped to the cash register.

"*Monsters & Maniacs*, Issue 48," he read.

Zandar turned to me. "You got Issue 48?"

"Have I got Issue 48?!" I practically shouted, ripping open

the exact plastic bin in which it was filed. I plucked the comic book out of its pile and held it up, triumphant. "You mean 'The Car of Tomorrow . . . It Seats Four AND *EATS MANY MORE!!!*' "

That's the one that was going to be the cover of my birthday cake!

"Bingo!" cried Gene the Bean.

"Way to go, Charley!" Zandar chimed in. "You want to sell it?"

Sell it?!

Zandar's question threw a bucket of cold water all over my excitement. I mean, Issue **48** is truly one my favorites. *Of all time!!*

But it was also my only chance to make any cash.

So, with a lump in my throat, I held Issue **48** for the last time. Zandar and Gene the Bean were respectfully quiet while I took an extra long look at its cover and traced my finger around the screaming faces of the victims being devoured by their family car.

And then, I handed it over.

As I wheeled home with what remained of my lifetime collection of *Monsters & Maniacs*, I was actually kind of glad that my comics weren't collectors' items—yet. And I was glad that in my pocket I had enough money to buy one box of cake mix and one can of frosting.

But that was all.

For every other part of my House of Horrors Birthday Party, I realized, I was going to have to get creative.

29

I crawled through our cupboards and closets and even climbed up into the attic to see what I could find to create spine-tingling, bone-chilling experiences at my party. I hauled out the Christmas decorations, the plastic turkey Mom sets out every Thanksgiving, and even the stuffed bunnies that Mom puts around the house when Easter comes.

Nothing scared me.

I pulled apart the fluffy cotton of the Christmas tree skirt that we use every year, because I thought that maybe the wispy cotton strands would remind people of cobwebs.

Not scary.

I tried wrapping the plastic turkey in gauze bandages, as if he'd been mummified instead of stuffed.

Not scary.

I even tried tying black ribbon around the necks of the Easter bunnies, thinking that I could hang them from the living room ceiling, as if they had been strung up as punishment for some grisly crime.

Interesting.

But not scary.

At school, however, I was in heaven. For the first time in my life, kids greeted me in the halls and waved to me on the playground. I felt like an Invisible Man who suddenly appears in the middle of a vast and appreciative crowd.

Donna and Dina and Dana cleared a place for me to sit with them at lunch, and Leo winked at me as he hobbled by on his crutches. Darryl challenged me to a chess game, which he won with seven moves, but I didn't care. Even Cougar and Scottie didn't smash me into walls anymore.

And Jennifer had trimmed her chopped-up hairdo into a tamer red halo. I thought it looked a lot better than it did before Cougar's stunt, but I wasn't going to tell her that; she was already behaving like a puppy who'd had too much coffee. Every day she'd rush up to my locker and give me the countdown.

"Three days to go, Charley! Then two! Then *one!* You must be so excited! Do you get rashes when you get excited? I do . . . *Look!*"

Jennifer almost succeeded in making me forget that, except for a devil's food cake with dark chocolate frosting, I would have nothing else to offer at my party.

The question of what I could *possibly* do to entertain my guests hung over my head like a sword suspended by dental floss, until finally, while walking Boing Boing past Garry's house late at night, I remembered how Garry had once offered to lend me his copy of *My Principal Is a Maniac!*

The thought of actually having to face Garry, though, absolutely terrified me. So I turned away and was heading for home when Garry's words popped back into my head again.

"Do *not* let fear rule your life, Charley."

So the next afternoon—on the day before my birthday—I took a deep breath and went over to Garry's.

When I walked into his backyard, he was at the redwood table, carefully painting a latex stab wound. It looked awesome.

Garry glanced up. I was sure he could hear my heart thumping against my ribs, that's how nervous I was. Once he saw it was me, Garry didn't say anything; he just went back to work. But he didn't ask me to leave, which I thought was a good sign.

"Did you make more scars and stuff?" I asked, indicating some of the other pieces he had lying around.

"I made what I could. Someone used up a lot of my latex," he answered quietly.

"Sorry," was all I could manage. Then I remembered why he was making all these wounds in the first place.

"Oh! When do you show your stuff? To the people at the theater place?"

"My audition?" he said. "My audition's tomorrow afternoon."

"Oh. Same as my party." I tried not to sound disappointed. Then I slapped on a smile and said, "You know you're invited."

"Thanks, but, like I said, I'm busy," he sighed. After he worked a little more, he added, "Besides . . . your mom doesn't want me around."

"Oh, she won't be there," I blurted out.

Garry looked up. "Huh?"

"Yeah. She has to work."

"But she's still letting you have a party?"

"She doesn't know."

That stumped Garry. "You're throwing your own birthday party?"

I nodded.

He shook his head. "That's not right. You . . . you shouldn't have to throw your own party. Not your Big One-Oh."

I could only shrug. "If I don't, who will?"

He looked at me for a long time, and in his eyes, I thought I saw the old Garry. My friend Garry.

It was just for a moment, but I'd swear it was there.

And later, when I asked to borrow *My Principal Is a Maniac!*, Garry loaned it to me, and I didn't even have to beg.

As I left with Garry's DVD in my hands, I had a really good feeling that his movie was going to save my party.

What I was planning to do was shut all the drapes in the house and lead my guests into the darkened living room. (That way they'd never see that there were no decorations.)

Then I'd put on *My Principal Is a Maniac!*, during which I would scream, *"Boo!"* or *"He's got a knife!"* before each of the scary parts and hope that my guests would jump and yelp in shock and surprise.

Afterward, I'd quickly feed them some cake and send them home before they realized what a dud my party turned out to be.

It wasn't much, but it just might fill a few hours.

* * *

I stopped inside the front door and slipped Garry's DVD under my sweatshirt; I didn't want to have to explain to Mom that I had disobeyed her order about going to Garry's. That's when I heard Lorena yell, *"Mom!"* from the living room.

"What?!" Mom answered from upstairs.

"What's wrong with the DVD player?" whined Lorena.

The blood drained from my face.

"Why?" said Mom, coming down the stairs. *"What's it doing?"*

"It won't eject my DVD of Mean Girls.*"*

"Well, don't use a screwdriver!" Mom cried. *"It's not ours."*

She was right. We didn't own our DVD player. Or our TV. Or our stereo. They were all on loan from Fittipaldi's Appliances.

"Well, I'll take it in and have the repair department take a look," Mom sighed, and that's when I lunged into the living room.

"YOU CAN'T!"

"Oh, Charley!" Mom gasped. "You scared me!"

"You can't take the DVD player back to the store. Not now!"

"I don't know why you care," Lorena sniffed. "It ate *my* DVD."

"Don't worry," Mom said as she unplugged the machine and wrapped up its cord. "I'll have it back by Tuesday." She patted me on the head as she exited, carrying with her the last hope of my salvation. Lorena followed her out.

Alone in the living room, I raised my fists over my head and shook them at heaven.

"Why?" I wanted to wail. *"Why me?"*

That evening I didn't want to arouse suspicion or draw attention to myself, so I made a simple spaghetti with meat sauce. See? Nothing special.

I thought I had succeeded in deceiving Lorena and Mom, but just before bedtime I turned and found Lorena leaning against my bedroom door with her arms crossed.

"You don't fool me for one second," she whispered with a sneer.

"Huh?"

"I hear things. I know what you're planning tomorrow."

"What?" I gasped, with my biggest, wide-eyed look. But I could tell that she wasn't buying it.

"Are you out of your mind, Charley? After what you did to the garage, you're gonna throw a party without Mom here?"

"But it's my Big One-Oh!" I pleaded.

"Do you know that Marci Liroff threw a pool party when her parents went to Las Vegas, and three hundred kids showed up? They broke the windows and threw the living room furniture into the pool!"

Under the circumstances, I would have voted for that kind of party, but who was I kidding? My friends could never lift our living room furniture.

"It won't be that kind of party," I insisted, struggling to keep my voice down so Mom wouldn't hear. "There's only eight people—nine, if you count me. We're just gonna talk and eat cake. I swear!"

"Yeeeesh!" Lorena snorted. "Boring."

"We'll have fun. You watch."

"Well, don't expect me to have anything to do with it. You are on your own."

She started to go, but then she leaned back in to add: "And Mom is *really* gonna kill you this time."

A HOUSE
OF HORRORS

30

I had bad dreams all night. I'd see visions of my classmates destroying our house, while my mom fell to her knees in the driveway, weeping wildly and tearing at her hair.

When Mom came in the next morning, I had to pretend that I was asleep. She kissed me on the forehead and whispered, "Hey, Birthday Boy," and I opened one eye.

"I'm sorry I've got to work today," Mom said.

In my best sleepy voice, I said, "How come you're sorry?"

"Because!" she laughed. "It's your special day."

"Oh. Yeah. I forgot," I croaked as I pulled the sheet up against my chin.

"When I'm home from work, we'll go out for burgers. Or maybe something fancier. You pick."

"We don't have to."

"Don't be silly," she said as she kissed my forehead again. "You're ten!"

She left my bedroom and shut the door. I listened as she descended the stairs. Listened as she made a quick inspection of the light switches and stove knobs in the kitchen. Listened as she went out the front door, started her car and drove away.

And then I sprang into action.

I threw back the bedsheets and jumped up, ready for battle. The night before, I had dressed in my street clothes so that I wouldn't waste a minute changing into them. I zipped into the bathroom and threw water on my face, and then I zoomed for the stairs, passing Lorena on the way.

"You're really gonna do this?" she asked sleepily.

"Try and stop me!" I yelled as I flew down to the kitchen.

The first thing I had to do was get the cake in the oven. I whizzed through the instructions on the box and poured the layers into two pans before it was even nine o'clock.

Because I wasn't going to be able to show *My Principal Is a Maniac!*, and I had no party games to play, I decided that I should turn my attention to decorating the house. I had kept a notepad under the covers in bed with me, and during the night I had written down every idea that popped into my mind, no matter how stupid it sounded.

First, I pulled out about twenty issues of *Monsters & Maniacs* and scattered them around the living room and dining room. I hoped they might spark conversations about gruesome and frightening topics:

"Oh! Look at this picture of a rotting zombie!"

"Wow, yeah! That reminds of the summer vacation my uncle lost a toe."

See? Something like that.

I kept popping into the kitchen, flicking on the light in the oven and looking through the hot little window to see how my cakes were doing. They were rising nicely, so I went back to "frightening-up" the house.

I hung a raincoat on a hanger and hooked it to the head of a floor mop. Then I floated them—facedown—in a tub full of water in the downstairs bathroom. Through the shower curtain it looked like somebody was drowning, with their hair floating around their head.

I hoped.

I tied a white bedsheet to a string which I led through a hook on the ceiling and tied to the bathroom doorknob. That way, when anybody pulled the door open, the string on the doorknob would make the sheet rise, and it would dance in front of them like a ghost.

Sort of.

I made devil's horns out of aluminum foil and tried to attach them to Boing Boing's head, but, after he shook them off eight times, I figured that he didn't want to be part of the decorations.

While I was racing around, I started to notice that, outside, the sky was darkening; black clouds were rolling in and blotting out the sun. I was beginning to worry that it might give my classmates an excuse to call and cancel. But then I walked into the kitchen, and I forgot all about the weather.

"WHAT ARE YOU DOING?!" I screamed at Lorena.

She had opened the oven and was sniffing my cakes.

"I'm just smelling them! Jeez. Don't split a gut."

"You opened the oven! The cakes could fall! What were you thinking . . . ?!"

But it was already too late.

As I got to Lorena's side, the two layers—puffy and perky one moment—suddenly sighed and collapsed to the bottoms of their pans, like they had lost all hope and had exhaled for the last time.

* * *

"I didn't know that about cakes," Lorena whimpered as we stood over my flat pastries.

"You don't know anything about *food!*" I fumed.

"Don't you have frosting? Frosting will make them tall."

"Yeah! About two inches tall!" I snapped. "Great. Just great! Instead of a birthday cake, I've got a birthday cookie."

"Can't you make another one?" Lorena asked.

I slowly sat down at the kitchen table and shook my head, finally overwhelmed and defeated by the events of the last four weeks.

"No," I mumbled in despair. "I can't make another one."

And then the doorbell rang.

We looked at each other.

"What time are your guests coming?" Lorena asked.

"Not for hours," I gulped. "Oh, no."

Lorena opened the front door in case one of my party guests was early and had to be sent home for a while. But that's not who was there.

A man in a silly polka-dotted orange jacket was standing on our porch holding on to a giant bunch of colored balloons that were swaying in the growing wind.

Boing Boing growled real low, but I wasn't sure if he was growling at the balloons or the Balloon Man's jacket.

"Charley Mapleweed?" the Balloon Man read from his clipboard.

"Maple*wood*," I said.

He reread his paper. "Oh, yeah. Maplewood."

He looked up, cleared his throat, and began to sing:

> *Happy Birthday! Happy Birthday, Charley!*
> *Celebrate cuz now you're ten!*
> *You'll never be this age again*
> *So Happy Happy Birthday, kid!*

Then he stuck the clipboard in my face and said, "Sign here, dude."

Lorena grabbed the balloons and gushed: "Cool! These'll brighten up the house!" I wanted to scream at her that I *didn't* want *to brighten up the house!*, but instead, I scratched my name on the Balloon Man's pad, and he left.

That's when, across the street, I saw Garry in his driveway. He was loading boxes into his car, and I remembered what he was heading off to. Without even thinking, I waved and shouted, "Good luck, Garry!"

He looked up. He didn't smile or anything. He just waved back, got into his car and drove off.

He was still mad. I could tell.

Lorena was inspecting the balloons, and when she found a gift card taped to one of the ribbons, she snatched it off and handed it to me.

"Read the card! Read the card!" Lorena had already forgotten that, only three minutes earlier, she had destroyed my birthday cake. But she always gets excited by things made of bright colors; I don't get it.

I opened the card, and when I saw what it said, I snorted, "Yeah. I bet."

"What? Who's it from? Who who who?" Lorena chanted.

I held up the card and read: "Dear Charley, Sorry about the mix-up. Your mom wrote me with the right date. Have a great Tenth Birthday. Love, Dad."

"No way! He finally got the day right," Lorena laughed.

I snarled at her: "He didn't get it right! Mom told him!"

She could see I was getting upset. "So what? At least you got balloons."

"Big deal!"

"You know, you can be such an ungrateful jerk," she exploded. "After all the crap that you've pulled, you should just be happy you're having a party!"

And that's when I lost it. All the frustrations and hopes and disappointments and sleepless nights of the last month came bubbling up, and I went *absolutely berserk!*

I leapt at the balloons in Lorena's hand, yanked them down and started punching them and kicking them and stomping and screaming, "I DON'T WANT A PARTY! I DON'T! I DON'T! I DON'T!!!"

My outburst freaked out Lorena, who yelled, "Charley!? What're you doing? Stop it!"

But I couldn't stop! And then, to make matters worse, I started to cry. "Send back the balloons! Send everybody home! I don't want a party ever, ever!" I wailed.

Lorena dropped to her knees and pinned my arms by my side.

"Charley! Charley! What's wrong? Tell me!" she said.

"A birthday . . . ," I choked out, ". . . a birthday is when you're special, and it's *your* day, and people come to see you."

"That's right," she nodded. "So?"

"But everybody's leaving! Or they're already gone," I cried.

"Who? Who's leaving?"

I pointed down the street. "Garry! I made him mad and he went away! And Mom's not here! And Dad doesn't remember unless somebody tells him to. They're all gone!"

By now, my whole body was shaking with sobs.

And that's when Lorena did something she hasn't done since I was about five.

She hugged me.

"*I'm* here, Charley!" she said. "I'm here."

"But you're my *sister*. You don't count."

That made Lorena laugh.

"Listen," she said, looking me in the face. "I owe you."

"For what?"

"You came running when Brad's hand got caught in my hair."

"But that's when I set the garage on fire," I reminded her, wiping the snot from my nose.

"It was the thought that counts," she said. "You did something nice for me."

I blinked at her. I had never heard my big sister talk to me like she cared. Not ever.

"So?" I shrugged.

"So. What can I do for your birthday?"

31

Dad's balloons hovered in a high corner of the kitchen ceiling as I raced around making final preparations.

By the time I spread the two cake layers with frosting and stacked them up, my cake was the thickness of a schoolbook. I made it a little more interesting by creating a little scene on top; I took the bag of plastic cowboys and horses that Mom had bought, and, with some of Lorena's red nail polish, I bloodied up a few of the cowboys, as if they had been in a shoot-out and had lost. Then I sawed a leg or a head off a few of the horses and scattered the body parts over the chocolate icing. I was going to have to warn people not to choke on them.

"How's this?" Lorena asked from the door.

I looked up, and I almost swallowed my tongue.

Lorena was wearing one of Mom's nicer dresses—Mom calls it a *cocktail dress;* she had on a blond wig that she once bought for a costume party, and she had on so much makeup that, at first, I thought she was wearing a mask.

"You don't look like Mom!" I cried.

"Your classmates don't know what Mom looks like."

"But you've gotta convince the parents! Or else they won't leave their kids here."

"And you only thought of that today?" Lorena was already sounding like Mom.

"You didn't offer until twenty minutes ago."

"Well, if I had more than twenty minutes, maybe I could make a convincing Mom. But as it is . . ."

The doorbell rang.

We froze.

It rang again.

I panicked.

"Go!" I pushed Lorena toward the stairs, hissing at her, "I can't have anybody see you!"

"Fine!" she hissed right back. "I don't want to be a part of your big fat lie anyway!"

And up the stairs she stomped.

The doorbell rang a third time, so I rushed to the front door. I heard a woman's voice on the other side asking, *"Darryl? Are you sure the invitation said today?"*

I was all ready to turn the knob and welcome my first guest when I realized that I didn't have any pants on. That's because I had almost completely changed into my nicer clothes after the balloons arrived, but—to keep my pants clean—I had laid them over the back of a chair until after I frosted the cake.

"How rude, Darryl. I don't think there's anyone at home," Darryl's mom was now saying.

I raced back in the kitchen, tripping over Boing Boing on the way, and yanked my pants off the kitchen chair. Hopping on one leg and then the other, I pulled them on as I lurched toward the front door, yelling, "Coming! I'm coming!"

I tucked in my shirt, zipped up my zipper, reached for the knob, jerked the front door open and shouted, "Darryl! You came!"

Darryl blinked. "Well. Yeah."

Darryl's mom was as thin and white as a sheet of paper. Her hair was tied back in a tight bun, and it seemed to pull her lips back along with it.

"You must be the Birthday Boy," she said. The way she smiled made smiling look like a lot of work.

"Yeah. I'm Charley. Charley Maplewood," I rattled nervously.

"We've been ringing this bell for ages," Darryl's mom said.

"Yeah. Sorry about that," I shrugged.

I noticed that she was looking over my head and into the house.

"Are we the first?" she asked.

"You sure are! Right on time. Come on in, Darryl!" I was anxious to get him in the house and close the door.

"One moment, Charley," Darryl's mom said, and I knew what was coming. "Where's your mother?"

"My mother?" I stalled, while my brain raced around in my skull yelling, *"Doomed! You're doomed!"*

"I assume there's going to be an adult at this party," Darryl's mom said.

"Sure is!" I smiled like a lunatic. "And there *is* an adult here. But she's . . . she's upstairs." I leaned toward Darryl's mom and whispered, "She's putting on her panty hose." Then I winked and added, "I'll tell her you said 'hi.' "

I took Darryl by the arm but Darryl's mom grabbed his other arm and, still smiling, said firmly, "I'd like to meet her."

"Oh! I bet you would!" I boomed.

"So?"

"And I bet she'd love to meet you."

"But?"

"But . . . she's shy."

"Oh," Darryl's mom was nodding now, not very happy about how this conversation was going. "You know, if there's some reason that your mother doesn't want to meet me, I'm not sure that I want to leave Darryl in these circumstances."

I was about to crack like a walnut, throw my hands up and confess, *"You're right! You got me! There's no adult here! This whole thing's a sham!"* But that's when I heard Lorena's voice calling from a window upstairs.

"Hello? Charley? Who's here?" Lorena was dropping her voice way down low, like she had been up all night screaming at a rock concert.

I ran out onto the front lawn, and Darryl and his mom followed me. We all turned to look up at Mom's bedroom window. There, behind one of Mom's lacy curtains, Lorena was waving like a beauty queen.

I was never so happy to see my sister in my life.

"Mrs. Maplewood!" I called up to her.

Darryl's mother turned to me. "You call your mother 'Mrs. Maplewood'?"

In a blind panic, I turned to Darryl. "What do you call yours?"

"Mom," he answered.

"MOM!" I called to the Creature in the Upstairs Window.

"Hello!" Lorena waved. "I'm Mrs. Karen Maplewood. Mother of Charley Maplewood. The Birthday Boy."

Darryl's mother squinted up and waved back. "Hello." Out

of the corner of her mouth, though, she muttered to Darryl, "Awful lot of makeup for this early in the day."

She caught me looking at her, and she knew she'd been overheard. So she patted her hair into place, pulled her car keys out of her purse and said, "Well . . . okay, then. I'll be back later, Darryl. You be a good boy."

She waved once more to Lorena and called, "Nice to meet you."

Lorena waved and smiled down like the Queen of England as she gushed, "Nooooo. The pleasure was entirely mine."

Once Darryl's mom walked away, he and I stood on my lawn for an embarrassed moment. I think that if there were a contest to decide who had the weirder mom, it would have been a toss-up.

Darryl thrust a colorfully wrapped present at me and said, "Ooops. Forgot. Happy Birthday."

He forgot? *I'm* the one who forgot! Because I'd been so crazy lately—and because this was my first party ever—it had completely slipped my mind that people would be bringing *ME* presents!

How cool is that?!

Just then a bolt of lightning crackled across the sky, and a booming thunderclap chased me and Darryl indoors.

It was like the sky was saying, *Oh, you're happy now, are you?*

Just wait.

32

Once it started to rain, it got a lot easier to fool everybody's parents.

They'd drive up, squint through their windshields at the house, and when they'd see Lorena waving from the upstairs window, that was enough to persuade them to release their child.

Dina, Donna and Dana arrived together. Then Jennifer pulled up right after Leo did, so she was able to hold an umbrella over his head as he hobbled on his crutches to the front porch.

Unfortunately, with every new arrival, it became more and more apparent how little I had to offer in the way of entertainment.

I tried to get people talking by pointing out *Monsters & Maniacs* covers and asking things like: "Do you think vampires are lucky to live forever?" and "I wonder if two-headed people go on double dates."

Jennifer jumped in with a few opinions, but nobody else responded. Instead, they stared gloomily from around the room, and, if not for the sound of thunder and rain outside, things would have been as quiet as a tomb.

"I thought this was gonna be scary," Darryl grumbled.

"I think that's coming," Jennifer burbled. She had managed to get her red hair under control by clipping it with about fifty bobby pins.

"I'm sure that *something's* coming," Leo added, sounding like the Class President that he is. But, because he was leaning on his crutches against a wall, he looked like he could just as easily walk out at a moment's notice.

"How come your birthday cake's so flat?" Donna asked from her spot at the dining table. Then she suddenly exclaimed, "Ew! Puke! There's headless horses in the frosting!"

That got a few people to rush over, asking, "Where?" But once they saw the teensy animal parts and the bloodied cowboys, they lost interest.

"I thought there was gonna be a movie," Dana said.

"What happened to the movie?" whined Dina.

"Yeah, Charley?" Leo tried to sound positive. "Let's see that movie, Buddy. Movie! Movie!"

The others picked up his chant, getting louder and louder, stomping and clapping, "Movie! Movie! MOVIE! MOVIE!"

"Oh, will you shut up!"

Lorena's bark made everyone spin around. I had forgotten that, without the benefit of the lace drapes, bad lighting and a distance of at least twenty feet, she looked pretty terrifying.

A few people gasped and turned away from the sight.

"You're not Mrs. Maplewood," Darryl guessed immediately.

"Give that boy a prize!" Lorena sneered. "No, I'm not Mrs. Maplewood, but I am bigger and meaner than any of you, so you do NOT want to mess with me." And as she said that last part, she yanked off her wig, releasing her wild hair.

"Are your parents *not* here?" Leo asked me.

"Uh . . . well . . . our Dad lives in Scotland . . . ," I started.

"Your mom, then! Is your *real* mom here?" Dina demanded.

"She, uh . . . she lives with us. Is that what you mean?"

Still inspecting the cake, Donna called, "Did an adult make this cake? Cuz it looks like it's poison."

"I'd better call my mom," Darryl said as he slid off the couch.

"Me, too."

"Me, too."

"I'm next!"

My party wasn't fifteen minutes old, and already the guests were fleeing. They rushed for the phone, where they wrestled for control of the handset, yelling and pushing.

The only one not in the crush was Jennifer, who stood in the middle of the room, soaking up everything that was happening.

"I'm having the time of my life, Charley," she shouted above all the noise.

Then an earsplitting whistle made everyone whip around to the doorway.

Cougar had arrived.

He dropped his whistling fingers from his lips and snickered, "Who invited all these losers?"

Behind him, Scottie shook off raindrops. "Yeah. Losers."

"Who invited *you*?" Lorena asked.

Cougar pointed to me. "Your idiot brother." He looked up and down at my sister in Mom's cocktail dress and said, "Whatever it is you're running for, sweetheart, I sure hope you win." He and Scottie hooted at that, but nobody else did.

"Y'know what? I don't need this," Lorena huffed. "Kill

each other for all I care." And with a flick of her hand, she turned and went back upstairs.

"Why are they here?" Jennifer whispered worriedly, nodding toward Cougar and Scottie.

"I . . . I sort of invited them," I stammered.

"After what they did?" she whimpered, and I watched the light fade from her eyes.

"Whoa, Jennifer!" Cougar strutted across the room. "What have you done to your hair?" She glared at him as he spun around to everybody else and demanded, "And what're the rest of you buttwipes doing?"

They all shrugged and mumbled, intimidated by Cougar's loud mouth.

"He doesn't have a scary movie," Dana said.

"I haven't been scared once," Dina added.

"I've been to bar mitzvahs that were scarier," Darryl snorted.

"Although this cake is scary," Donna said, pointing at it nervously.

Cougar pulled a balloon down, bit its neck off and inhaled the helium inside. Then, in a very, very high voice, he peeped, "You guys are all such weenies!"

That got people laughing.

"And he . . ." Cougar tweeted, pointing at me, ". . . he's the birthday weenie! The biggest weenie of all!"

That's when things started to fall apart. Suddenly everybody forgot about calling their parents; instead, they wanted to bite their own balloon and talk in a funny voice, too. They grabbed the balloon ribbons and leapt up at the ceiling. They stood on chairs, walked across the sofa, and climbed on the dining room table.

"That's mine!"

"I had the red one!"

"You wish!"

"Gimme! Gimme! Gimme! GIMME!"

And then the first balloon popped.

Dina squealed, *"Eeek!"* but that only made everybody else laugh. So, in one fateful moment, everybody went from wanting to hold a balloon to wanting to kill one.

Within minutes, my guests were bouncing up and down on the sofa and stabbing at balloons with plastic cake forks.

Pop! Blam! POW! It sounded like a gunfight had erupted in my house.

Dina turned on the stereo, found a radio station blaring rock music, and cranked it way up. Then, as Leo was hopping around on his cast and bobbing his head in tempo to the blaring stereo, Donna and Dana started dancing on the furniture.

Scottie was entertaining himself in the kitchen by dropping pennies into the disposal and listening to them tumble and crunch, while Cougar was running around the room, flicking the lights on off on off on off, like he was creating his own strobe light show.

When they saw me in the doorway, Cougar yelled, "What happened to your House of Horrors, Jerkface?" and Scottie barked, "Boo!"

Darryl had locked himself in the bathroom (the ghost-sheet-on-a-string hadn't bothered him one bit), and Jennifer was pouting in the corner chair, still fuming because Cougar and Scottie had shown up.

I was running around yelling, "Cut that out! Put that down! Don't walk on the couch! At least take your shoes off!" when suddenly the doorbell rang.

I quickly counted heads. One, two, three, four, five, six, seven, eight. All my guests had arrived. Mom was at work. So who was at the door?

Rain was pouring down in sheets, and even though it was mid-afternoon, the sky was midnight dark when I ripped the front door open.

"What do you want?" I snapped. Then I stopped. And I looked up . . . up . . . up.

Because there was a giant on my front porch.

The wide brim of the hat on his head cast a shadow over his features, but there was no mistaking this creature's size: he was HUGE. Then a lightning bolt zapped across the heavens, and for one awful moment, I saw his face.

And I clutched at my throat in terror!

For I was looking into the face of the ugliest creature I had ever seen; a face full of pain and malice, a face without mercy, covered with scars and stitches and warts. In a voice that seemed to rise from the deepest pits of hell, he spoke:

"Helloooo . . . Charley."

33

I opened my mouth to scream, but this monster . . . this *MANIAC* clapped his hand over my mouth. He leaned down, his red, runny eyes just inches away from mine. Then he snarled:

"Make one sound, and I will rip your head from your body."

And if it's possible to pass out while standing up, that's just what I did.

I offered no resistance when the Monster lifted his hand from my mouth and steered me across the entry until we were just around the corner from the living room.

He leaned down to my ear and hissed, "You know what I *don't* want you to do?"

I shook my head frantically, which started my teeth chattering.

He twisted my head around the door frame so that I was just peeking into the chaos raging in the living room. "I don't want you to look away."

I gulped. I held my breath.

And this is what I saw.

Darryl had come out of the bathroom and was sulking on the sofa; Jennifer was reading a copy of *Monsters & Maniacs*; and Donna, Dina, Dana and Leo were still dancing when Cougar and Scottie raced into the room, dripping wet from their fight over the kitchen sink sprayer.

"This party suuuuuuucks!" Cougar shouted.

"YEAH!" almost everyone agreed.

"What happened to the House of Horrors, huh?" someone shouted.

"Ooh, I'm soooo scared!" said another voice.

And people laughed.

Cougar thrust a hand into the air. "Who wants to go slip and slide on the lawn?"

I was amazed to see that—except for Darryl and Jennifer—no one hesitated to wave their hands overhead and squeal, "Me! Yay! Slip and slide!" They all turned to rush for the door.

But then they skidded to a stop.

Because the Monster was now standing in the living room. He'd pulled his hat low, so they couldn't see the hideous face I'd just seen.

Outside, lightning bolts zapped and threw quick, spooky shadows on the walls. Thunder rattled our windows. And for a long time, nobody spoke. My guests giggled, nervous and embarrassed. They looked around, their eyes asking each other, *Who is this guy?*

Cougar finally broke the silence with a snicker: "Who're you?"

In low, horrid tones, the Monster rumbled, "The Birthday Boy asked me to drop by and eat some of his . . ." He stopped and cleared his throat. "I mean, *meet* some of his class-mates."

And, saying that, he tossed the hat off his head and lifted his face into the light just as a thunderclap exploded outside.

Dina, Dana and Donna squealed all together, and everybody stopped breathing.

Yes! I thought; *Behold the face of evil!*

Since Cougar was in front of the pack, I could see his face the clearest. And it went white.

"Uh. Charley's here. Somewhere," he stammered. Then he tried to leave the room, but the Monster stopped him with a finger to his chest.

"Charley? Ah," said the Monster. "I've already seen him."

By now, Darryl was cowering on the couch, but Jennifer was leaning forward, her eyes alive with fear and excitement.

"Charley didn't look so good," the Monster continued. "But that's only one man's opinion." He slipped a hand into his enormous black overcoat. "I'd like to know *WHAT YOU THINK!*"

And as he said that, from out of his overcoat he pulled . . .

. . . *my head!!!*

I'm serious! He was holding my head by my hair, *and it had been cut off at the neck!* I gagged in horror! My own head—the one still on my shoulders—was unable to make any sense of *my head in the living room!*

Everybody's jaw dropped down so far that I could see who still had their tonsils and who didn't. Then, in one big tidal wave of noise, they all screamed together.

The Monster took one step toward my classmates and they lost it.

Shrieking and wailing, they scattered. They dove under tables, squeezed behind the couch and crawled into cabinets.

The Monster tipped over the chairs that Dina and Dana had found to hide under; they fled like cockroaches, but like cockroaches who could screech like car alarms. They ran into the dining room, where they collided with Donna, who was running the other way. They all agreed to run in the same direction while the Monster chased them around and around my pathetic birthday cake. Finally, he cut off any possible exit, and he cornered them.

Then when he opened his mouth and revealed that he had *two long, glistening fangs*, their shrieking was so supersonic that it shattered a window above the side table.

Leo and Darryl were fighting over who'd get to hide in the hall closet when the Monster suddenly appeared behind them, grabbed each one by a shoulder and spun them around. They flattened themselves against the wall, whimpering, "No no no, please, no no no!" Then the Monster opened the palm of his right hand and held it up for them to see that—there! embedded in the flesh of his palm!—was a set *of gnashing teeth!*

Darryl's hair shot straight up.

But—and this surprised me—it was Leo who fainted. Right into Darryl's arms.

I hope you won't think I'm being cruel when I tell you that I had to clap my hand over my mouth to keep from laughing. It's not always fun to get scared yourself, but, boy oh boy, it can be really hilarious to watch other people losing their minds!

As I was coming back to my senses, I looked down to find that Boing Boing had joined me in the entryway, watching all the hysteria with a bored look. Unlike his response to the Balloon Man earlier, Boing Boing wasn't barking at the Monster.

And I thought, *That's strange. He usually barks at strangers.*

And then my brain, which only minutes before had been shocked into blubbering stupidity, began to send me a message: *Maybe this Monster wasn't a stranger.*

Maybe he was somebody who knew me.

Somebody who knew it was my birthday.

Somebody who just happened to have a copy of my head lying around.

Do I need to go on?

Cougar and Scottie had been dashing from room to room, trying to outrun the Monster. After they swung the kitchen door in his face, they gained a few precious seconds, and, in that time, they both had the bright idea to hide under the living room sofa. They dropped to the floor at opposite ends of the couch and squeezed underneath until they boinked heads in the middle.

"Ow!" Scottie whined.

"Shh!" Cougar shushed hysterically, hoping that they could escape the Monster's detection.

But, in addition to worrying about death-by-Monster, Scottie had another problem.

What very few people know is that when Scottie gets upset, he throws up easily. Since he's embarrassed to talk about it, Scottie had never told Cougar.

But Cougar was about to find out.

Cougar twisted his head the moment he recognized the sound that Scottie was making—the sound a dog makes after eating grass.

"Oh, no! Scottie, no!" hissed Cougar. "You're not really gonna . . ."

"Merp!" Scottie belched in warning. And then, just as Scottie lost his lunch—*SPEW!!*—into Cougar's face, the Monster seized Cougar's ankles. "NOOOOOOooooo!" Cougar wailed, his nails scratching at the floorboards as he was dragged out from under the sofa.

Wearing Scottie's lunchtime burrito all over his head, Cougar now cowered at the feet of the Monster. He was squirming and shrieking, "DON'T EAT ME! PLEASE DON'T EAT ME!" over and over.

Everyone stopped hiding or screaming, and they all turned to watch our class bully begging for his life, writhing around on the living room rug. The Monster, towering over Cougar, threw back his head and laughed a horrible laugh, and when he was done, everything went strangely quiet.

Because now everyone was staring at Jennifer.

She was standing in the middle of the living room, holding my severed head by the hair.

"This . . . is . . . so . . . *COOL*," she marveled. Then she tapped my skull and watched my smile swing back and forth.

Donna and Dina and Dana, whose faces were drenched with tears and snot and runny makeup, recoiled with a collective, "*Gag!*"

Scottie, peeking out from under the sofa, winced as he continued to wipe spit-up from the sides of his mouth.

Darryl, who had finally gotten Leo to his feet, shook his head and moaned: "Oh. That's not right."

And Leo, who was just coming around, fainted again.

But Jennifer wagged a finger at the Monster and said, "You almost had me." And when she pinched my head's "nose" between two fingers, I got so giddy with excitement that I jumped out of my hiding place.

"BOO!" I shouted.

Which only made everybody scream again.

After they got over the initial shock and Leo regained consciousness, everybody decided that they were furious with me.

Dana said, "Charley, you're a creep!"

Darryl muttered: "Thanks a lot, Charley. Now I'll need double sessions with my therapist."

And Donna walked right up and yelled in my face (my real one), "Charley Maplewood, you scared us half to death!"

Then Jennifer topped them all by crying out: "And wasn't it *awesome?!*"

Everybody stopped. And nobody said, "No."

Instead, they looked around, trying to figure out what everyone else thought. And when they began to nod and snicker, it seemed that what everyone else thought was, *"Yeah. I guess it was."*

Leo started to laugh . . . Leo, who had spent most of the time unconscious.

And Dina joined him. (I think Dina likes Leo and was trying to score points with him; but, still—she laughed.)

Dana was next. Then Donna. And even Darryl, who was
fighting it with all his might, began his funny snorty-laugh.

Scottie, who was so relieved not to be smacked for having
hurled on Cougar, laughed. And so did Jennifer.

This is what everybody came for! I thought as I looked
around. *Fun!*

"So who's your Monster, Charley?" Leo shouted.

"Oh!" I took charge of my birthday party, the way I always
imagined that hosts are supposed to. "Meet Garry Quarky."

I suddenly had a momentary doubt, so I spun around.

"It *is* you, isn't it?"

Garry reached up and ripped off his ugly face in one swift
move, and everyone gasped: "Whoa!"

"It's me," Garry smiled, freed from all that latex.

And, as Garry peeled the warts and hairs and scars from
his head and his hands, everybody pushed closer, wanting to
see what made a man into a monster.

Cougar, however, didn't join them. Instead, he snuck up
alongside me.

"Hey, man," he whispered. "You got any clean underwear?"

I looked at him and crinkled up my nose. "You don't
mean . . . ?"

He nodded.

Finally, my guests began to enjoy themselves. We laughed
about the stupid birthday cake I had made. We laughed

about Scottie throwing up and Leo passing out. And we laughed about how we had all behaved when Garry first appeared.

"You should've seen your face!"

"My face? What about *your* face?!"

"And the way you screamed!"

"The way *I* screamed!"

We went on like that until Garry reached into the pocket of the Monster's overcoat and pulled out a perfectly painted *hand.*

"Coooool," everyone agreed.

"Remember this?" Garry asked me.

And I did. I excitedly explained to everybody how, even before he cast my face, Garry had cast my hand.

"Hey," Cougar piped up. "Is your sister still upstairs?"

"Yeah," I said. "Why?"

I yelled up to Lorena to come down.

"I'm in the shower!" she yelled back.

"It's an emergency!" I insisted. "You have to come *now!*"

We were all gathered around the kitchen chopping block when Lorena burst into the kitchen. She was wrapped in her bathrobe, dripping wet and hopping mad.

"*What?!* What is going on down here, Charley?! Even in the shower, I can hear screaming and furniture crashing and . . ."

She slowed down, because she saw that I had my hand laid out on the cutting board. And that Jennifer had a meat cleaver raised up over it.

"NOW what are you doing?!" Lorena squeaked.

"You're just in time," I snickered. "Check this out!"

And that's when Jennifer swung the cleaver down on my "hand"—*THUNK!*—chopping it off at the wrist. It dropped to the floor and rolled to a stop at Lorena's feet.

I'm willing to bet that Lorena's scream interrupted television reception in six states.

My guests and I were in the middle of the longest, loudest laugh that any of us had ever laughed, when suddenly—in the next split second—the laughter turned to *shrieks of horror!*

Because that's when our front door *BLASTED!!* wide open.

I thought it was a bomb. I really did.

Instead, a whole *army* of policemen and policewomen poured into the house, waving guns and shouting: "DOWN ON THE FLOOR!! EVERYBODY DOWN!!"

They were holding the leashes of snarling police dogs who barked and snapped ferociously at us.

And then, as if that weren't horrible enough, the *back* door exploded in, and *even more* police swarmed in, surrounding us and shouting *even louder!* By now there were about a dozen cops and a wild pack of dogs, and, between all *their* yelling and barking and *our* screaming, there was a terrible racket.

We held our trembling hands over our heads, knelt on the floor and tried not to cry.

Why? I wanted to yell. *What did we do wrong?*

But as I lifted my head to speak, Mom—my real mom, not the phony Lorena mom—walked in the front door, drenched by the rain that was falling outside. She was shaking her head with disappointment and fury.

Did Mom call the cops? I wondered. *Wow. She must be mad.*

And that made it official: my Big One-Oh House of Horrors Birthday Party had come to an end.

THE
PARTY'S OVER

34

That's my story; I told it just like that.

When I finished, I looked around at the faces of all the people and animals squeezed into my living room.

There were Mom and Garry and Lorena and Boing Boing. There was Mrs. Cleveland, her arms folded in judgement.

There were my party guests and their parents, who had come to pick up their kids, only to find them surrounded by most of the Fresno Police Department, who had also listened to my saga.

So had seven ambulance drivers who had been waiting outside, ready to transport any casualties to the nearest hospital. I had even shared my story with our neighbors from way down the block who we hardly even know but who come running whenever fire trucks or police cars arrive.

See, what I hadn't known was that—while I was in the middle of my party—Mrs. Cleveland was in the middle of a meltdown.

Ever since I had burned our garage, I guess Mrs. Cleveland had decided there was no evil deed that I was not capable of. So when she heard popping noises coming from our house, she didn't stop to think that they might be balloons exploding.

Oh, no.

She assumed that I had somehow gotten my hands on a gun. And that I was using it.

When Mrs. Cleveland saw the lights in our house flashing on and off, she didn't stop to think that Cougar might be flicking them on and off, keeping time with the radio music.

Oh, no.

She assumed that my victims were desperately signalling for help.

And when Mrs. Cleveland heard people shrieking at the tops of their lungs, she didn't stop to think. Instead, she picked up the phone and called the cops.

And the hospitals.

And the fire department.

And Mom at work.

In all the time it took to tell my story, not one of those people in my living room moved. Not even the dogs. And now that I had run out of things to say, they all stared back at me in silence.

Finally, I turned to Mom and shrugged. "So, can you see now? How one thing leads to another?"

Mom was still pretty stunned. She had already had to deal with a lot that afternoon, and after the police had kicked in our front door and back door, I was sure that she was going to make me live in a cardboard box in the backyard for the rest of my childhood.

But I had to make her understand.

"I'm really, really sorry," I said. "I didn't mean for it to happen like this. But I didn't know what to do. I had no one to help me. And nowhere to turn." I started to choke up, but I was determined to finish. "And besides, it's . . . it's my Big One-Oh."

I think I might have been able to control myself if only Mom hadn't nodded. But, once she did, once she showed that she understood, I couldn't help it. And, as much as I tried to stop them, I could feel the salty tears leaking out of the corners of my eyes and rolling down my cheeks.

There was a long moment when I felt about as dumb and embarrassed as a kid can feel without totally exploding with shame, but then I realized that people around the room were sniffling, too. And it wasn't just my family or the kids from my school.

No.

Cops were clearing their throats. Policewomen were swiping at their eyes. Darryl's mom even took a pill, she was so moved.

Finally Mrs. Cleveland, with tears streaming down her face, broke the awful silence by throwing a hand up into the air and crying, "Lord Almighty!"

We all turned to her. I was afraid she was going to announce that I had a nuclear weapon or something, but instead she surprised us all by shouting, "Hasn't this child suffered enough?"

And, in that moment, I could've kissed her.

Because, you know what? Everybody agreed with her: I *had* suffered enough.

"Poor kid!"

"What a nightmare!"

"All that he went through!"

"And it's his Big One-Oh!"

And that changed everything. People turned to each other and began chattering away. Neighbors and policemen and classmates and ambulance drivers all seemed to forget that they didn't really know each other, and they behaved as if they were at . . . well, *at a party.*

Mom blew her nose on a cake napkin, stood and turned to the crowd. "Hello, everyone?" she called.

"Hello!" they all called back.

"As you have heard," she said, "it's my son's birthday. And I'm so glad that you could all make it."

Everybody laughed. Even I laughed.

"I'm just so sorry that I don't have any cake to offer you," she said.

"Oh!" Garry called out. "I've taken care of that."

By the time Garry had run back to his place and returned with his cake, people had started to help Mom and me clean up.

A few of the policemen put the doors back on their hinges, and some of the parents mopped up the mud that had been tracked in when the house was stormed.

Tables and chairs were turned over and put back in place; one of the ambulance drivers gave Scottie something to settle his stomach; and I took Cougar upstairs and loaned him a pair of clean underwear.

Garry's cake was amazing. It was decorated all over with rubber fingers and noses and eyeballs staring up out of the frosting. When Mom saw it, I thought that she'd freak out, but instead she exclaimed, "Did you make that?!"

Garry nodded. "Blame Charley. He once told me that if I

could reach the sink, I could cook, so . . ." He gave a little shrug.

Mom patted her chest the way she does when she's trying not to cry. She looked at Garry gratefully, and she quietly said, "Thank you."

They stayed like that, looking at each other, until Lorena waved a hand between their faces and said, "Whaddya say we cut that cake?"

Everybody gathered around and sang "Happy Birthday to Charley!" Mom took a picture as I blew out the ten candles and everybody cheered.

I sliced the first piece, and people screamed in surprise when the cake spurted "blood" that tasted like strawberry syrup. But then they all laughed about having been scared, and they clapped Garry on the back, saying things like, "Oh, man! You really got me!"

It was everything a birthday party's supposed to be.

And it was mine.

It was early evening by the time everybody left. The sky was clear after the rainstorm, and the sun was setting behind a fiery red fan of clouds.

The policemen and policewomen shook my hand, wished me a Happy Big One-Oh, and then they left without arresting anyone. The ambulances followed the patrol cars out of the traffic circle, and the neighbors-we-never-met wandered back to their houses at the far end of the street.

Mrs. Cleveland hugged me before she took her walking stick and started her nightly patrol.

Leo tried to high-five me, but I didn't know how to respond, so he and Scottie and Cougar and even Darryl crowded around and gave me a crash course.

When they left together, Dina and Dana and Donna pecked me on the cheek, and they waved out the window until their car disappeared down the block.

When Jennifer stepped up, I extended my hand, like I wanted to shake. She looked disappointed that she wasn't going to get a kiss like the other girls, but she shook my hand anyway. Then when she saw what I had slipped into her palm, she gasped, "Oh! Oh! Oh!"

She held up my latex eyeball—the one Garry had given me—and she examined it like she was looking at the world's largest diamond. She smiled so hard I was afraid her braces would *sproing!* off her teeth. Her eyes got shiny, and she threw her arms around my neck, hugged me and whispered in my ear, "Thank you, Charley! Thank you, thank you, thank you!!"

"No," I said. "Thank *you.*"

I stood on the front lawn until the last cars pulled away. Mom and Lorena had gone inside, and I thought I was alone.

But when I turned around, Garry was there. He had cleaned off his face and changed out of the high boots that had made him so tall when he was my Monster.

"Hi," I said.

"Hi."

"You really scared my friends."

He smiled and kind of looked down—really bashful, really pleased. "Y'think?"

And I could tell that Garry wasn't thinking about North Carolina anymore. Hearing my classmates' screams and watching them running around like drunk chickens had made him a really happy man.

Then I remembered something.

"Hey! What happened at your audition?"

"Oh. I called them and told them I'd come at another time."

"Why?" I gasped.

" '*Why?*' " he laughed. "Because. It's not every day my friend turns ten."

On a day of so many memorable moments—some of them horrible, most of them wonderful—that's the one that stands out.

My friend. Garry had said the words. *My friend.*

And that was big.

Bigger than the Big One-Oh.

I put my head down as Garry and I headed back to my house so Garry wouldn't see that my eyes were getting wet again.

"You like Chinese food?" he asked.

"Lots."

"Cuz I had an idea: it's your birthday. You don't want to have to cook. You think your mom would like it if I go and pick up some chop suey?"

"Yeah. Mom likes Chinese food even more than I do."

And so that's what we did.

After we ate our Chinese food and opened our fortune cook-ies (mine said: "You will get some new clothes," which doesn't sound like a fortune handed down from ancient China), Lorena and I cleaned up while Mom and Garry talked and laughed at the dining room table.

When we got into the kitchen, Lorena rolled her eyes and groaned, "Now we'll never get rid of him."

I'm hoping that she's right.

It had been a long day, and I was feeling really wiped out, but I wasn't ready for my birthday to end. That's why I came up here to my bedroom, pulled out my Birthday Notebook, and, with Boing Boing resting his head in my lap, I wrote down everything that happened, just like I told everybody it did.

I also wrote a thank-you note to Dad. Not just for the balloons and the issues of *Monsters & Maniacs*. But also for sending me the wrong birthday card on the wrong date and for writing the ten words that had changed my life: *"What are you going to do for your big day?"*

I still had one more thing to do. I flipped to the middle of my Birthday Notebook, and I reread what I had written under THINGS TO DO FOR MY PARTY:

#3 was FIND A THEME. I found a pretty good one, don't you think?

#2 was WATCH PEOPLE WITH FRIENDS TO LEARN HOW. I had done a lot of watching. And a lot of learning.

And finally, #1 was MAKE FRIENDS. I'll have to wait until school on Monday before I can be sure of the others, but right now, I'm feeling pretty good about Garry.

And, y'know, it's funny, looking at that list now, I feel like I wrote it another lifetime ago. Because all of a sudden, as late as it is and as tired as I am, I feel like a different person.

I feel like I'm less afraid of the world than I used to be.

I feel taller.

Stronger.

Maybe a little wiser, even.

But, c'mon! Is that so surprising?

After all . . .

I *am* 10.